D0854956

TAUNTON
DUX FEMINA FACTI
COHANNET
A TOWN 1639. A CITY 1864.

Keepers of the Gate

Keepers of the Gate

STEVEN G. SPRUILL

DOUBLEDAY & COMPANY, INC.
GARDEN CITY, NEW YORK 1977

All of the characters in the book are fictitious, and any resemblance to actual persons, living or dead, is purely coincidental.

ISBN: 0-385-12420-1
Library of Congress Catalog Card Number 76-18367

Printed in the United States of America
First Edition

To Nancy Lyon

Keepers of the Gate

BOOK I

Earth

One

Captain Jared Hiller, A.S.N., was asleep in his bridge pod when the Protep vessel was sighted. He dreamed of Earth and of the spacious private room that went with the four gold stripes on his sleeve. In his dream he was lying in bed savoring the aroma of simileggs sputtering on the autochef. It felt good to rest on sheets again and to contemplate idly a ceiling which was an adequate distance above his head. Then a bell started ringing somewhere and the simileggs smelled suddenly of ammonium carbonate. Hiller forced his eyes open and groped automatically for the stimulant cut-off, as sensors just above his eyes gently increased the light inside the pod. He squinted anyway when the leaves of the pod popped open, then scowled to cover the laxness in his face as the flat webfoam curved into a chair beneath him.

"Protep vessel, sir," the exec whispered.

Hiller grunted and swung his chair around to the bank of screens, automatically noting the positions of the crew around the cramped circular bridge. The alien ship was close, incredibly close astern; a sleek sharp-nosed vessel of the planetfall class—about the size of a Terran cruiser. He had seen one like it on the Protep embassy pad outside Washington.

"Why wasn't I called sooner?"

"It warped in, sir."

"How the hell . . . ?" Hiller felt four pairs of eyes swing toward him; strained bloodshot eyes. Scared eyes. A week of silent running deeper and deeper into the forbidden zone had cornered each for too long with his own thoughts.

"Very well," he said. "Maintain silence in all systems." The need to whisper robbed his voice of any reassurance it might have given. He made a show of yawning and was rewarded by a drop in young Edwards' shoulders and a knowing smile from his exec.

Hiller turned back to the screen. The Protep cruiser was still holding position, its foreshortened port side bathed in white brilliance from Epsilon Eridani. In the bottom of the screen, the glistening blue-white surface of Eridani's third planet barely seemed to curve against the black of space. Hiller shook his head. How in God's name could a ship warp in this close to a planet? If an Earth vessel had tried it, it might have materialized inside the planet's core. He mentally filed it away. There were more pressing problems—like whether the Proteps were being fooled by the asteroid disguise of his ship. Every conceivable detail had been attended to—they had precisely calculated the slow tumble inward from the asteroid belt outside Eridani's sixth planet. Everything but the silent satellite cameras was shut down. There was even a realistic meteor burn along one side of the ship to account for how a chunk of rock might have been knocked loose from the belt. But it all seemed a naked farce now. The alien vessel slipped onto the bow screens as the squat Earth ship turned on her axis; Hiller could almost feel the silent lash of probes crisscrossing the *Trojan*'s rough hull. He wondered if he was seeing the last thing Ketterly had seen aboard *Trojan*'s sister, the *Hound,* two years ago, or the last thing seen by half a dozen Earth ships swallowed by space in the five years since First Contact.

"If we only knew what they've got," the exec muttered. Hiller nodded. A technology that could pop a ship into normal space 270 miles planetside might also be able to pick up pinhead-sized lenses on the surface of their ship or hear them whispering through a half mile of space and three feet of rock. He turned to the science officer.

"Do we have enough shots yet?"

There was a pause and Hiller saw fear and duty struggle on the man's face; saw the bump of his Adam's apple as he swallowed hard.

"Not really, Captain. We haven't been close-in long enough for a good three-sixty. The cameras will only pick up cities at under three hundred miles, and . . ." Hiller waved the man to silence and swiveled toward the engineer's station, but his eye was caught by the stiff posture of the signal officer, a big man named York. York wore the look of a man about to do something, but he flushed under Hiller's gaze and settled back against his chair. Hiller's mind tagged it and moved on—the man might have to be relieved soon.

"Kuznetsov, have you plotted a warp out of here?"

"Days ago, sir." The stocky engineer patted the console beside his chair and grinned, revealing a huge gap between his two front teeth. "Not that I'm in any hurry to leave," he added. Kuznetsov's smile spread to the others, except York, and Hiller could feel the tension ebb.

"It's dropping back," the exec whispered suddenly. Hiller followed her gaze to the bilge screen fed by a lens on the *Trojan*'s underbelly and watched as the Protep ship dwindled and stretched from a bright spot to a shaft. It was turning planetside, he realized with delight.

The sudden clatter of the *Trojan*'s norm-space radio froze Hiller's hand in the thumbs-up position for one brief instant before he could react. Then he twisted toward York and lunged out of his seat, but Kuznetsov got there first, hurling the signalman to the floor. York lay where he fell, his face a white mask around unfocused eyes, while the others stared at him in disbelief.

"Edwards, get him to quarters. If he gives you trouble, stun him. Kuznetsov, stand by to warp out." Hiller's voice was a whip, driving the others into motion. Edwards muscled the unresisting signal officer through a hatch in the bridge floor, Kuznetsov swung back to his console, and the exec snatched up the all-systems headphones. Hiller watched with a sick feeling as the Protep ship swung back to bear on the *Trojan*, then ballooned into a gleaming mass that filled the stern screen. He could even make out a silver seven-point star set into her prow above the strange lettering.

"Heavy probes, Captain," the exec reported. "We're getting 2,017 megacycles off the hull and something moving very fast through the bridge—tagged neutrinos, I think. By now they should know that our little rock is hollow."

"Very well. Engineer, warp us out."

"Aye, aye." Kuznetsov hit the central relay controlling the Opperman drive and Hiller steeled himself for the wrenching in his stomach that always accompanied a hyperspace jump. Nothing happened. The Protep cruiser still filled the rear screen.

"God's eyes," muttered the exec.

"Take the conn," Hiller snapped as he jumped out of his chair and cycled open the engine room hatch. It irised shut behind him, cutting off the bridge, and he hurried, stooping, down the short passage which forked at the crew's quarters and the engine room. At the fork he nearly stumbled over something; for a long instant he stared at Edwards' body. The eyes were open and the head was at an odd angle, one ear nearly touching the shoulder. Hiller cursed and plunged through the engine room doors. In the dim emergency lighting he could see the outer service panel of the Opperman drive lying on the floor. An acrid smell, like burnt insulation, hit his nostrils. He turned to the intercom and his eye was caught by the red light above the maintenance airlock, which signaled that the lock was in use. One of the two pressure suits beside the lock was gone—York had left the ship.

Hiller slammed the intercom switch. "Shut it down," he yelled. Then there was a blinding flash. Pain seared through Hiller and broke into a thousand madly spinning pinwheels which careened outward into total blackness.

Two

Hiller sat quietly in the heat at one of the small outer tables of the Aerie and sipped whiskey. Once, his mild acrophobia would have kept him away from the low railing, but the new eye had changed all that. He tipped his chair back and peered over the edge. The side of the Alliance Building plunged downward into a patchwork of rooftops packed together at various heights stretching outward to where the massive plastite citydome curved into the ground. A tangle of short causeways sprouted from different levels to span the chasms between buildings. There was scarcely room, Hiller reflected, for a person to plummet between the buildings, miss the network of causeways and hit the concrete two hundred stories below. A man had done it yesterday, though, stepping carefully over the wrought-iron rail and disappearing tight-lipped. Two weeks before that, a woman had jumped rather than stepped—the difference between agony and quick death, since it carried her across onto the hopter pads atop the McArthur building only four stories down. The medics had rushed her off, but the railings stayed low and everyone knew why. Hiller stared down into the labyrinth of two- and three-foot-wide alleys at ground level, where the man had fallen —dusky littered passages touched only by a half hour of dome-filtered twilight either side of noon. The alleys were all that remained of the streets and parks of Old Washington. Below them, reinforced basement levels groped around a multi-layered subway system to depths where ceilings sweated and stank of mold.

Hiller drew back from the railing with a touch of regret. Something in the neuro-circuits of the new eye censored and expunged whatever had once lurched in his stomach at a view from high places. He lifted his glass and drained it in mock salute to the departed spirit. Then he crushed the glass in his right hand and gazed incuriously at the unmarked synthetic flesh of his palm. Working the eye the way they'd taught him at the clinic, he peered through the sleeve of his V-coat, through the plastic and cord mesh, to where bunched servomotors clustered around steel shafts. It was a good arm, a good eye, a good leg, a good right lung. . . .

Hiller jabbed at the button set into the middle of his table; held it down until a burly waiter pushed toward him across the crowded roof. The waiter frowned at the bright shards of glass on the table, raised his eyes to Hiller's face, and then thought better of whatever he'd been about to say.

"Another," Hiller said. Idly he scanned the needler under the man's V-coat, reading the charge indicator on the butt of the weapon. Full. The waiter moved off, a flash of red against the subtle décor of the crowd, and returned a moment later with the whiskey and a hand vac-unit. With his left hand Hiller awkwardly fished out his wallet and thumbed a crisp blue note onto the table.

"That should cover the glass, too."

The waiter nodded and deftly swept up the litter. When he was gone, Hiller looked up at the slightly brighter circle in the yellow-green haze above the dome. About two o'clock—time for the city to flush its hordes into the drop and jump chutes, funneling one shift out and the next in to still-warm seats. He watched as the rooftops began to launch their hoptercab swarms into arcs carefully computed somewhere in the bowels of the city. It reminded him of some mystical insect rite—blue and green bottle flies dancing over garbage. Beyond the dome his eye caught a vertical column of disturbed air streaking upward through the haze south of the city. The heat wake of a navy ship blasting off from Andrews. Hiller's right hand curled around the railing and squeezed until the metal started to bend.

"That's quite impressive."

Hiller let go of the rail and turned. Oddly, his first impression was of how he must look to her—a stocky middle-aged man with a stomach going soft and untidy red hair. He found himself wishing suddenly that he had followed the advice of the plastic surgeons and had the patches of real skin left on his jaw permanently depilated.

"May I?"

Hiller indicated the chair across from him and watched the graceful way she sat; felt her knee touch his under the table. He drew away.

"You're Captain Hiller, aren't you?"

"No."

She raised a neatly penciled eyebrow and waited.

"I'm *Mister* Hiller. Mr. Jared you-can-call-me-Jad Hiller."

"I thought it was customary for retired officers to retain their titles."

"Who the hell are you?"

She smiled and Hiller felt himself flush, as though he'd been caught bluffing at poker.

"My name is Anne. Anne Cantrell."

"And why are you carrying a knife, Anne Cantrell?"

Her hand moved unconsciously toward her breasts and away again. "That's also very good," she said. "Just how much *can* you see?"

"Alas, only your bones and other hard things," Hiller said with a smile. "You didn't answer my question."

"That's horrible. You mean you don't see my face when you look at me? Only my . . . my skull?"

"I see what I want to see. It's all very complicated. For example, if I liked I could see that you have a very nice mouth, dark eyes, and lots of brown hair—all of it yours."

"Can you see me with a perfectly straight nose?"

"How did you break it?"

She looked disappointed. "I was covering a 'right-to-bear'

demonstration on the DAR Building and one of the women mistook me for an antibirther, the stupid bitch. That's why I carry a knife now. Damn it, if they can do a job like that on your face, why can't they straighten out my nose?"

"Are you?"

"Am I what?"

"Are you an antibirther?"

"Of course. But not when I'm working." She leaned over and pushed the button.

"Ms. Cantrell, I don't want to be rude, but . . ."

"Aren't you even curious about how I know your name and . . . the other things?"

"No. You are a reporter for one of the synpapes, you're packing a wire in your waistband, and . . ."

"It's turned off . . ."

". . . and I don't feel like talking."

"I don't believe you."

The red-coated waiter appeared by the table and sized her up approvingly.

"I'll have scotch," she said crisply, without glancing at him. He looked at Hiller and moved off, shaking his head.

"Look, Cap—Mr. Hiller. I've seen you here every day for the past four weeks, sitting at this same table, sipping yeast-vat whiskey and never smiling. You've already smiled once since I sat down, and I'm going to see that you do it a few more times before I leave."

"Just because I don't smile, doesn't mean I'm not happy. Maybe they fixed my jaw so it hurts to smile. I've already had more press coverage than I needed, so if you'll just sort of shove off . . ."

"I'm not working now and this is not for the synpapes. But if you really want me to I'll leave after I've had my drink."

"And who'll decide if I really want you to?"

"I will, of course."

The waiter brought her drink and she paid the exact amount.

"I think you got a raw deal," she said after a few swallows. Hiller just looked at her. "I know," she went on, "you think I don't know the half of it, but I've looked into it—really looked into it. Your ship—the *Trojan*—blew up suddenly while on some kind of mission off Epsilon Eridani III. Cause of the explosion, unknown. Survivors, one."

"More like a half."

"Is that what you really think?" Her eyes held his.

"Only when I'm sober," he said after a moment. She nodded and went on.

"A dramatic rescue by the Alliance cruiser *Littlejohn*, which happened to be hovering a thousand kilometers away. Five months in a hospital and another six in a rehab clinic."

Hiller shifted uncomfortably in his seat. "Listen, it's been great going over the old memories, but . . ."

"Jad, why did they put you out? Your eye; your arm and leg—they're better than flesh and blood. . . ."

"That's what the brochures say."

"Then why?"

Hiller looked down into his drink while his mind took him back to the admiral's office—to that day against which the next weeks were such poor insulation. He'd stood there, fresh out of rehab, savoring the scent of lunar tobacco in stained oak walls, trying to guess how many inches of bronze-colored carpet were pushing up around the sensors in his new foot, while the admiral fiddled with papers on his desk. He'd sensed that something was wrong; read his name upside down at thirty paces on the top of an unsigned letter of resignation. After that there had been only the tightness in his throat and the pressure back of his real eye while the admiral droned on: "Outstanding service record . . . unfortunate and tragic accident . . . regrettable memory loss . . . psychological side effects. . . security risk . . . full pension and continuance of living arrangements . . ."

Hiller looked up from his drink. "Because I failed."

"Failed?"

"Lost a navy ship. Blew my mission."

"Which was to get as close as possible to the Protep planet and bring home some solid intelligence that we could work with."

"Print that and they'll make the rest of you like your nose, only they won't leave it as neat."

"I'm not going to print it, but it's true, and will you stop with my nose." Hiller smiled. "That's it," she said. "When you smile, you feel better."

"I thought it was the other way around."

"That's because you're an external." She made it sound like a bad word.

"An external?"

"A person who believes he is at the mercy of things. I'm an internal."

"You believe that things are at the mercy of you."

"Yes."

Hiller nodded and swirled the whiskey on his tongue, savoring its bite and the burn it made going down his throat. "I notice you've finished your scotch."

"Oh, damn!" She stared at her glass. "I wasn't going to gulp it this time. Does that mean you want me to go?"

Hiller said nothing; gazed at her.

"Good," she said. "Jad, what happened up there?"

Hiller watched an orange hoptercab skim across just beneath the dome on a cross-city run. For a moment it looked like it would collide with an upward-arcing blue model, but at the last instant the second craft dipped gracefully beneath it.

"I don't know," he said. "I don't remember. We were coasting in, beginning to get some good shots . . ." He stopped guiltily.

"C'mon, Jad. You've got to trust me."

"Why? Why do I have to trust you?" He stared at her, feeling peeved at the conspiratorial mood she'd put him in. They were like two kids playing at spies.

"I don't know. That's just what they always say—'you've got to trust me.'" She said it theatrically and then laughed. "I guess you don't have to trust me."

"Look, let's just forget it. All right?"

"Sure." She looked at him. "What are you going to do?"

"Well, I'm going to sit here for another hour until it gets dark and I get drunk enough to go back to my room."

"That's . . ."

"Disgusting?"

"Well, no . . ."

Hiller said, "Ms. Cantrell, this has been amusing. Fun, even. But you have an interest that my old colleagues in the business would consider unhealthy. You can carry the reporter bit too far."

"What do you mean, reporter bit? I told you . . ."

"I have to believe you have an instinctive reporter's interest in all this," Hiller said. "We've been losing ships at a time when Earth needs ships. Something is throwing us out of space at a time when too many people are breathing out for the rest to breathe in." He gestured at the packed rooftop and the city below. "I tried to play my little part in getting us some room, and I failed. That's all. End of story."

"I told you that I don't want a story," she finished as though he had not interrupted.

"Then what do you want? I can't believe . . ."

"What's wrong?" She followed his gaze to a tall blond man who had just appeared out of the roof chute. He was dressed in a conservative blue V-coat and checked trousers, and was looking around the rooftop with casual but professional thoroughness.

"It can't be," Hiller muttered. He shoved up from the table and moved into the crowd, his eyes fixed on the man.

"Wait a minute . . ." Anne said.

But Hiller and the blond man were gone, as surely as if they had melted into the roof.

Three

As Hiller stood, the blond man's head turned toward him and for an instant their eyes locked. In that instant, Hiller knew, even though it could not possibly be, that the man was Martin Pavel. He thought he saw the faintest flicker of emotion on the man's face—surprise or fear. Then Pavel turned and vanished back into the drop chute. Hiller tried to get through the press of people standing between the tables. A woman bumped him and dropped her drink, cursing. Her escort reached out for his arm, but Hiller shoved past and swung into the drop chute as the next platform fell level with the roof. Watching the floors drift upward in front of him, Hiller tried to guess Pavel's next move; decided that he would try to widen his lead as fast as possible. He stepped off at the 180th and caught a glimpse of checkered trouser leg disappearing into an express drop down the hall. He moved fast but the door slid shut before he could reach it, and he had to wait for another.

When one finally popped open, Hiller jumped on; felt his ribs suck at his stomach as the cage began to plummet. The main concourse and principal network of causeways were located on the twentieth floor where the express drops ended. Pavel had a ten-second jump on him, more than enough in which to disappear. Hiller practiced switching his vision into the body heat frequencies while the express cage finished its plunge. Across from him hovered the vague reddish heat-ghosts of two previous riders.

One had stood more quietly than the other; Hiller guessed from the outline and the extra heat that it had been a fat man.

The doors swung open and Hiller winced at the swarm of dancing red images before quickly damping them out. Unless Pavel got out of the crowds, his heat image would be useless for tracking. As he stepped onto the crowded concourse, Hiller let his mind float; tried to pick a direction. He struck off to his left, covering the area in front of him with quick swings of his eyes. Suddenly something registered—a steel door labeled "Police Only," set into the tiled mosaic on his left. Hiller stopped and heat-scanned the coating of grime and smudged fingerprints on the door. Most were cold but one set had a faint shimmer about them. After a look up and down the concourse, he twisted the handle gently and slipped through into cool darkness. His right eye adapted instantly; fed him a quick gestalt of a dusty stairwell lit by a red dirt-encrusted exit sign. He eased the door shut and listened. Something small scurried a few levels down, and then there was silence except for the steady plink of dripping water. He switched to heat frequencies and looked first down and then up. It was faint, but there: the barest whisp of a heat trail.

Suddenly there was a new sound. Hiller listened, holding in his breath, until it came again from above him—the stealthy shift of a shoe against the metal staircase, added this time to a gentle sough of wind in and out of lungs; controlled panting. His scalp prickled. The man was close—just above him.

Hiller reached over, pushed open the door and moved his feet a bit, backing quietly against a corner of the landing as the door clicked shut. There was a wait of perhaps five seconds and then a rush of footsteps—going upward. Hiller cursed and rushed after the man, stopping short when he saw heat traces on the exit door of the third landing. He pushed through into the hallway and ducked away from the blur of movement at the corner of his eye. Something crashed against his spine, inches below the vital spot on his neck, driving him to one knee and sending shock waves through his back.

Hiller lurched up, grabbed for Pavel's head, and missed,

catching him in a bear hug instead. His right arm tightened and mental warnings flashed, as Pavel gave a strangled grunt. Hiller eased off at once and the other man struck out in a frenzy. Hiller clawed the top of Pavel's coat, behind the neck, grasping as much material as possible before Pavel broke his grip and tore free, lunging into a crowd of onlookers. Hiller tried to follow, but Pavel swung into an open drop chute and disappeared. After a few minutes of scrambling between floors, Hiller admitted defeat and turned his attention to the scrap of cloth he'd torn from Pavel's back. There was a piece of label from an expensive clothier and below that the thing he had hoped for—a fragment of laundry tag. It was printed with a small design and the words "—stwood Arms."

Hiller walked to a wall phone and punched the display for "E" but there was no Eastwood Arms in Washington. That left Westwood Arms, and Hiller whistled when he saw the address. Half an hour later by A-level subway he was there, standing in a glittering lobby hung with twentieth century Danish chandeliers and cooled an extra few degrees by lightly scented mist from two fountains. Hiller avoided the main desk, which jutted into the lobby like the prow of a ship, and walked to a blue-painted door lettered "gentlemen." It was locked. Without looking around, he gripped the knob in his right hand and twisted until he heard a soft pop.

Hiller stepped inside and moved quickly to the mirror hung over a marble washbasin. He looked worse than he had feared—nowhere near well enough to wheedle information out of the lean sharp-eyed man at the desk. Threats were out, too—he'd counted three black-suited security guards from the agency of Brown and Clauswell.

Hiller found some depilatory cream in a dispenser and set about making his face look respectable. When he finished, he combed his hair and looked critically at the results. With the patches of red stubble gone, the smooth scar along his jaw was barely visible, but the effect was still grim. He tried a smile and succeeded only in baring his teeth. He shook his head and walked back out into the lobby, noting the positions of the security men. As he strolled up to the desk, the clerk eyed him with discreet thoroughness.

"May I help you?"

"I'm here to see Martin Pavel."

"There is no one here by that name," the clerk said without hesitation.

"He could be using a different name. Perhaps if I described him . . . ?"

"May I ask who you are?"

Hiller pulled out his wallet, withdrew his I.D., and flicked it at the clerk, who made no attempt to scan it but simply held out his hand. Hiller grunted and laid the plastic card on the desk beside his wallet.

"Captain Jared Hiller—Naval Intelligence?"

"That's right," Hiller said, hoping.

"Retired, I see."

Hiller said nothing and the clerk handed the card back. "Then your business is not official."

Hiller looked around and lowered his voice. "This is a delicate matter and the Navy cannot afford to be officially involved."

"I see." The clerk's voice was neutral.

"The man I am looking for is about two meters tall, blond-haired, muscular." Hiller watched the other man's eyes.

"I'm sorry. . . ."

Hiller opened his wallet and withdrew a five-credit note.

"On the other hand, the man you describe could be our Mr. Stanek," the clerk said as he smoothly palmed the bill. "He has the same first name. . . ."

"Which apartment?"

"The penthouse, but . . ."

"I'll find my own way up."

"Captain, that is quite out of the question. Without a personal key, the lift will not even go to the penthouse."

Hiller nodded. "Perhaps I'll wait for him here, then. Thanks for the information." He pocketed his wallet and walked away, pretending to admire one of the fountains. The clerk watched him for a moment and then turned away to take care of a tenant.

Hiller checked the security men, walked casually to the old-style elevator, and got on as another man stepped off. As soon as the doors slid shut, he pressed the top numbered button and withdrew the small knife-like tool which he still carried out of habit. He had the cover off the control box and was studying the wiring when the elevator slowed suddenly. Hiller checked the light; the elevator was only halfway up. The door slid open; a blue-coated security man nodded at him and stepped on. Hiller caught his arm halfway to the needler on his belt, jerked him off balance, and hit him with one steel finger behind the ear. The man dropped to his knees, sighed, and fell forward against Hiller's legs. Hiller eased him to the floor, stuck the needler inside his coat, and turned back to the panel as the elevator began to rise again. He had the wiring solved with ten floors yet to go, took the lock off the top circuit, and quickly pushed the penthouse button. The elevator stopped at the floor below and Hiller rolled the snoring guard into the hallway before continuing to the top.

The doors opened onto a foyer piled deep in rich blue carpet. Hiller finished replacing the control coverplate and stepped out, looking quickly around. There was no one in the foyer. A more leisurely inspection revealed another Danish chandelier, only a little smaller than the one in the lobby, subdued blue and gold wallpaper, and a heavy-looking door. Hiller carefully examined the chandelier until he found the peeper. It was a conventional tracking model that would follow him as he made a circuit of the foyer—he'd installed plenty of them himself in his time. It would not be a danger so long as someone somewhere was not watching its screen.

The door was thick and fitted perfectly into the wall, leaving no cracks. There was an identiplate centered in it which would respond only to the programmed palmprint. Tampering with it would require time and tools that he didn't have. . . . There was a conventional lock above the doorknob, and as Hiller bent close to inspect it, his eye caught a faint beam of light from the keyhole. Pressing the eye against the lock, Hiller focused on a view of something on the apartment wall opposite the door. He had just realized with a shock what it was when the elevator doors slipped open behind him. He had time to stand up and turn around before Pavel—or Stanek—stepped into the foyer.

"It's been a long time, Martin," Hiller said. Stanek made a move back toward the elevator and then stopped, letting the door slide shut behind him.

"You've made a mistake, friend," he said softly.

Hiller walked over to him, scanned the coat for hidden weapons, and let his eyes linger on the left arm. With a cold feeling in his stomach, he realized that he had been right.

"There's no mistake; only a small mystery," Hiller said. "I'm beginning to guess why you're pretending not to know me."

"I don't know you, and you don't know me." Hiller noted the faint sheen on the man's forehead, the clenching of his jaw.

"A lot has happened since Mount Goodsir," Hiller said, "but I haven't gone senile. Let's talk about it, Martin—I'm not out to get you, I just want to know."

"You're raving."

"I'm going to find out anyway, now that I've seen you. It's important to me—surely you can understand that." Hiller searched the other man's face, wondering if he could be wrong. It had all happened so long ago. . . .

The elevator door slid open again. Hiller reached inside his coat and then reluctantly let his hand drop as four black-coated men stepped out, needlers first. One was the guard Hiller had stunned. "Don't even twitch," he said. "Are you okay, Mr. Stanek?"

"Quite." Stanek smiled grimly. "I'd advise you to co-operate with these men." He nodded and the security guards moved quickly, boxing Hiller between them.

"I'd like my needler back, butt first and slowly."

Hiller complied. The man shoved it into his belt and walked around behind him, taking the wrist of Hiller's right hand. "I've got a little something for you to remember me by, friend," he said. "Sort of a trade, you might say." Using his other arm for leverage the man twisted and jerked upward, grunting with the effort, but nothing happened. Hiller's arm stayed stiff at his side. The man looked at him uncertainly.

"Suppose we just settle for me leaving quietly," Hiller said. The guard looked at Stanek, who studied Hiller a moment and then nodded thoughtfully. The guard indicated the elevator with mock politeness and Hiller got on, followed by the others.

"Forget these delusions of yours," Stanek said as the doors were closing. "Senility's better than not growing old."

When the guards had ushered him out a side door of the lobby and he stood alone in the narrow alley between buildings, Hiller let his mind go back to the thing he had seen through the keyhole. A fragment of memory burned again into his mind, as it had for that instant outside Stanek's door, before he had been interrupted. He squeezed his eyes shut and leaned against the wall in sudden dizziness.

The memory was of the prow of a Protep ship looming in a viewscreen. Every detail stood out in strange clarity—the wash of white light from Epsilon Eridani, the alien lettering, and the silver seven-point star. The star like the one in Stanek's apartment.

Four

When Hiller got back to his apartment, Anne was waiting for him. She was sitting with her back against his door, hugging her knees.

"What are you doing here?" he asked.

She just looked at him as though he'd said something foolish.

"How did you know where I live?"

"Really! When you were in Intelligence, didn't you ever just look someone up in the phone book? Or did you always have to get it on the sly, asking the delivery boy or something?"

"I don't have a phone; I hate phones."

"Do you want to talk about it?"

Hiller sighed. "Wait here." He turned and walked back down the hall. He rode the elevator down to the lobby and got a vidphone booth after waiting only five minutes. Slipping his plastic card into the slot, he punched in a number and waited some more, tapping his fingers against the glass. Finally the screen lit up with a puffy unshaven face which glared at him for a second and then softened.

"Hiller, is that you, you sonofabitch?"

"It's me."

The face split into a grin. "Well I'll be damned. Hey, I tried to see you at the clinic but the bastards wouldn't let me in. I've been real worried about you. . . ."

"I'm fine, Sam."

"Yeah, I can see that." Sam eyed the pickup carefully. "I don't even see the scars. They said you'd lost some skin off your face and . . . and an eye, and some other things."

"Listen, Sam, I need a favor."

"Sure, name it."

"I want you to check someone out for me; a synpape reporter named Anne Cantrell."

"Right now?"

"If you can."

Sam nodded and swiveled around, revealing a broad white-shirted back with a patch of sweat in the middle despite the near frigid air in which he worked. Hiller could make out the dull gray of the C.I.B. computers in the background. He watched while Sam pecked at a keyboard.

"Anne with an e and Cantrell with two l's?" he asked over his shoulder.

"Try it and see."

Thirty seconds passed while the computer hummed and the printout chattered. Then Sam swung around again and held up a sheet for Hiller to read. He scanned it, looking mainly at background information and searching for the little asterisks that signaled a security entry somewhere else in the computer. There were none. Toward the bottom of the sheet was a cryptic entry which read "Detained R.T.B. disturbance. Treated fractured nasal septum. Released." Hiller smiled, then grew serious again as he read the final entry—about her job.

"Thanks, Sam."

"Sure. When are we getting together?"

"Soon."

The sheet dropped from in front of Sam's face, revealing a hurt expression. "Aw, Hiller. . . ."

"Really. I'll bring a bottle and we'll talk." Hiller punched the disconnect and pushed past the line of tenants waiting for the booth. After a stop at the liquor store in the next building he went back up to his apartment. Anne was still sitting where he had left her.

"Actually," she said, "I got the address from the bartender at the Aerie."

Hiller nodded, took the hand she offered in his left one, and pulled her to her feet. "I guess you can help me kill this," he said gruffly, showing her the bottle.

"Quit acting like you're sorry to see me. Just because you rushed off in the middle of my sentence doesn't mean you don't like me. Besides, if you want me to go away, why are you still holding my hand?" She smiled sweetly. Hiller dropped her hand and opened the door to his apartment.

"I can explain about rushing off," he said. She followed him in and looked around. It was a large single room, befitting Hiller's rank. A huge untidy assortment of rocks bent a long table downward in the middle and there were even more stones scattered on wall shelves. Soil from half a dozen planets and moons still clung to the rocks and lent a pleasant earthy smell to the place. On every wall but the kitchen, stark depth photos of alien landscapes left only narrow strips of plasterite showing. There was a fold-down bed, an autochef, a command chair that Hiller had cadged from an obsolete naval tanker, and a desk littered with strange tools. The over-all effect was of a museum's private chamber—a place where the curator could live with his work. Anne ran her fingers over a collection of small stones, while Hiller watched, his face still.

"What's this red one?" When he didn't answer right away she looked up.

"I found it on the slopes of Nix Olympica. It stood out like a jewel on the dark lava."

"Mars." She smiled.

"Okay. So you can buy a hunk of Mars rock in any curio shop—school kids collect them like sky-hockey cards. To me it's something else."

She moved quickly over to the autochef. "I'll bet you're starved. Why don't you fix us a drink. I'll whip up something while you explain why you stood me up."

Hiller opened a cabinet and took out two glasses. "I hardly stood you up. . . ."

"Hold it. How do you work this thing?" She was poking randomly at the console, a perplexed look on her face. Hiller walked over quickly. "I'll take care of it. You pour the drinks." He dialed a couple of fish-cake dinners, trying to remember whether he'd stocked the chef with high- or low-grade soyeast. After the rye whiskey it probably wouldn't matter, he decided. She handed him the drink and he settled into the form chair while she perched on the edge of his bed.

"I guess I owe you an explanation," he said, wondering if it was a rationalization for his need to talk. "Besides, I need someone to tell me I'm not crazy. It's odd. The minute I saw him, everything came rushing back." Anne waited, swirling her drink, until he tipped his chair back and continued, eyes on the ceiling.

"Twenty-five years ago when I was twenty-two—after college and before the Navy—I decided it was time for a little adventure. Time to see what was outside the citydomes besides a lot of poisonous air. I'd heard that there were a few places, like parts of Canada, where you could still breathe open air, if conditions were right. I went into the south part of Old Alberta and knocked around for a while in a place called Calgary, near a slope of the Rockies. I'd get a mask and back pack and go out of the dome during the days, scratching for limestone and seeing what I could see."

"Limestone?"

"A local factory used it to make that fungicide they're always spraying in the lower subway tunnels. Anyway, I'd scratch days and drink up the profits at night with a bunch of roughnecks who made a permanent living that way. It began to wear thin and I was thinking of getting on back to the States when Stanek came along. Only he was calling himself Pavel in those days. Said he wanted some men with mountain-climbing experience to help carry equipment on an expedition to Mount Goodsir, a little ways north. The pay was good, so six of us signed on." Hiller chuckled. "One climber and five penniless liars of which I counted myself the boldest. We all watched the guy who could climb and we did all right. The equipment was bulky but light—parts of a research station, Stanek said. But at night, after we'd make camp and crawl into our air tents, I'd see him go off by himself with a gadget the size of a breadbox. I've never seen anything like it before or since, and I never did figure out why he'd sneak off with it like that. Stanek was a pretty cold guy; not chatty. Kept to himself and only spoke to us to give orders—always in a polite way."

"Dinner-r is ready," announced the autochef in scratchy tones. Hiller got up and shoved a circular floor rug aside with his foot. He whistled a high note and a metal table and two chairs unfolded out of the floor. Anne looked surprised.

"The receiver is keyed to that pitch on an internal circuit from that wall switch," he explained, pointing; "but you can bypass it once you get the knack." He put the steaming fish-cakes on the table and they sat down. Anne applied herself to the meal with a seriousness that amused Hiller.

"How long since you've eaten?" he asked.

"I always wolf," she said around a mouthful of food. "Go on with your story."

"Well, one morning Stanek seemed excited. We were only about halfway as high as he'd said we were going, but he said this was it—our campsite would be just the place for his research station. We all thought it was odd, since we were on the edge of a pretty narrow ridge. We'd passed a flatter spot just the day before. But he paid us off and told us to take enough supplies for ourselves and go on back." Hiller grew suddenly intent, laying down his fork and staring at his plate. "That's when he fell off the cliff."

Anne stopped chewing.

"I don't know how it happened, exactly, but he tried to step around some stuff we had piled next to the edge and the rock broke off under his feet. We got to him as fast as we could, roping over the cliff and then scrambling down another steep slope covered with little rocks. We must have each taken a dozen nasty spills of our own. On the way down I found his arm." Hiller looked at his food as if it had suddenly turned loathsome. "It was torn off at the shoulder and completely mangled. Since there was no chance of reattachment, I just left it. Stanek was nearly dead when we got to him—mask knocked off, face broken up; lots of other things, too. I don't know how he lived long enough for a spray of Cauterol on his shoulder stump, let alone for the hopter flight back to Calgary. We left him at Mercy Hospital. I took my credits and winged it back to the States. I'd had my adventure, and I was ready to forget it and stick to something safe for a while."

"Like becoming a navy pilot?" Anne said.

Hiller nodded, missing the irony. "I haven't thought about it more than a dozen times since it happened. It's all there, though."

Anne finished and patted her lips with the napkin, eying Hiller's half-empty plate. "This man you followed from the Aerie; I didn't get a good look at him, but he seemed to have two arms. So I guess one was mechanical, huh?"

Hiller shook his head. "It was real flesh and blood. I got two close looks at it and there were no steel shafts or servomotors—just normal bones." He told her about the chase; how he'd lost Stanek and found him again.

"Maybe he had a transplant or something," she said when he had finished.

"That wasn't possible then and it's still not—not with any degree of success. Even when they avoid tissue-rejection problems, the new arm's hardly more than a hunk of meat. It's much simpler and better to tie on one of these," he said, tapping his own arm, "with xylon nerve and vessel interfaces. Then you can do all kinds of marvelous tricks—everything but feel. Besides, I'm telling you, that was Stanek's arm and not somebody else's; right down to the blond hair, the shape of the fingers—everything."

Anne picked up their dishes and scraped Hiller's half-eaten fish-cake into the autochef's reconverter, before stacking the plates in the sonic bath. "All right," she said when she had finished. "Then there's something else you've got to consider."

"I know. Any sane person would conclude that he'd made a mistake—that Stanek only looks like Pavel. But I've got a theory about sanity going back to when I was broken in as an agent: Being sane means seeing what you're supposed to see and not seeing what isn't supposed to be there. By that definition, I've been trained into insanity. I believe that Stanek is Pavel."

Anne put a hand on his shoulder. Her fingers felt cool against the base of his neck. "Jad, I won't say that I understand how you feel, because I couldn't—not fully. But are you sure you're not seeing this because you want to see it? I mean, if Pavel can somehow regain a human arm after losing one, then so can you. A thing like that could affect anyone's objectivity."

"Damn it, don't you think I know that?" Hiller snapped. Then he patted her hand contritely and got up. "I won't say I have no doubts; only that I've got to find out for sure." He walked to the liquor cabinet and poured himself another whiskey, ignoring the hot needles that seemed to be pricking his face. Anne covered her glass when he held out the bottle and watched as he dropped heavily into the chair. The dull beat of someone's bass speakers began to pound half a tune down through the ceiling.

"All right," she said at last. "But you've already said the arm is neither mechanical nor a transplant. So what does that leave us besides him just deciding to regrow his own arm?"

Hiller laughed. "Now you see? That's what I mean about sanity. Suppose he did just regrow his own arm?"

"Jared Hiller, I'm taking that stuff away from you." She made a half playful grab at his glass.

"I'm serious. Let's just think about it for a minute. Human medical science cannot have produced what I saw. What does that leave us?"

She stared at him a moment. "The Proteps?"

"Right. There's something I haven't mentioned yet—something I shouldn't be talking about." She shot him a warning look and he held up a hand. "But of course I'm going to. There is a seven-point silver star on a wall of Stanek's apartment."

"So?"

"It's the Protep emblem. I—I've seen it on their embassy gate," Hiller improvised. Anne looked at him for a moment.

"I've been by there. I had to do an article on them once. I never saw anything like that."

"It must have been somewhere else, then," he said, not looking at her. "Anyway, I'm sure of it."

"But it proves nothing. Maybe Stanek saw it and admired the

design. Maybe it's got nothing at all to do with the Proteps—there's nothing particularly extraordinary or sacred about the design, any more than . . . polka dots."

"Maybe," Hiller agreed, looking at her again. "But maybe there IS some connection. We know that the Protep technology is almost certainly ahead of ours. The design of their ships at the embassy proves that. . . ." Another fragment of memory teased Hiller, this time of a voice whispering, *It warped in, sir.*

"Is something wrong?"

"No . . . I . . . Just . . ." Hiller shook his head. "Excuse me a minute." He got up and walked unsteadily to the small bathroom at the back of his apartment. He closed the door and bent over the sink, splashing cold water on his face until the tap cut off and the red "empty" light flashed above the meter. Then he toweled off and opened the door, almost running into Anne. Her hands clutched at his ribs through the thin shirt and her eyes held a glint of fear.

"Jared, are you all right? Shall I call a medic?"

"Too much to drink," he said.

Suddenly the feel of her hands against him did something and he kissed her on the mouth. She stiffened for only a second and then moved against him, bringing her fingers up behind to play in the hair at his neck. He felt himself tremble; took her by the shoulders and gently moved her away. They looked at each other for a moment and Hiller felt something pass between them. Then Anne laughed shakily.

"What did you take in there?"

"Nothing."

"Well, I'll have some of it too."

He walked past her into the room and sat down, this time on the bed. He could feel his heart pounding against the cellulon of his right lung. She joined him, sitting at the other end of the bed and studying him.

"I was talking about the Proteps," he said, trying to ignore the lame sound of it. "What if there is some sort of arrangement between Stanek and them? They're pretty aloof to humans as a rule; but what if Stanek is different for some reason? Anne, we don't know what they're capable of."

"That's the first time you've said my name."

"What if, sometime after they first landed five years ago, they found Stanek, needed him for something, and offered him a new arm in return?"

"I like it."

"You do?"

"When you say my name."

Hiller felt himself blush. "Damn it, will you be serious?"

"Jared, this isn't the Navy any more—you're not about to ship out to space for a year. It isn't intelligence work either. You can have friends now. Be with other people—like them; even do some *using* back and forth if you want to."

She slid across the bed toward him.

When it was over, Hiller lay beside her and tried to think. The blower above the bed kicked to life and stirred the whisp of her hair that had drifted across his chest. A man and woman passed his apartment arguing in shrill voices which receded until a door slammed.

"There's something else I didn't tell you," he said after a long time.

"Mmmm; what?"

"The thing between Stanek and me; it happened twenty-five years ago."

"That's what you said."

"What I didn't say is that Stanek hasn't aged a single day since."

Five

"It's farfetched." Anne studied a piece of toast before popping it into her mouth.

"So you've been telling me—for the last three days."

She leaned her elbows on the breakfast table and watched as Hiller poured two cups of cafee from the tap on the autochef. "I'm sorry. I guess I have been a drag."

He set a steaming mug in front of her and sat down. It had been a good three days; he hated to break it off. "Would you like some sugar?"

"You're kidding. Real sugar?"

"I found a vacuum tin of it in one of the abandoned survey stations on Luna. It probably goes back to the 1990 expedition." Air hissed as Hiller twisted the opener; he put a touch of the fine crystals on his tongue as Anne watched intently. She let him pour a generous stream into her cup before raising her hand.

"M-m-m. What are you going to do next?"

Hiller set the tin down, leaving his own cafee black, and wrapped a hand around the cup until his palm turned pink from the heat. "This and that," he answered at last.

She looked down at her plate. "I get it. You're getting ready to ditch me so you can go after Stanek. But what if I offer to come along and help you?" She kept her face down but raised her eyes.

Hiller shook his head.

"And if I demand to come along and help you?"

"It just wouldn't work."

"Right. I might sneeze while you're listening through a door, or pass out, or get myself kidnaped like in the trivees."

"Something like that."

"That's stupid. That's really stupid." She shoved back from the table and stalked over to the bed, straightening the sheets with angry jerks. "You think I'm some dumb boob; me, Anne Cantrell, the best damn synpaper in Washington."

Hiller got up and walked over to her. "I think it's time you started looking for another job," he said gently. She stared at him and then sank down on the bed.

"You checked."

"I'm not a dumb boob either."

"Okay," she said after a minute. "So I don't work for the synpapes any more. I've got money—I'm not trying to freeload off you. Besides, I'm good at finding out things. You're going to need someone. . . ."

Hiller saw that her eyes were moist. He sat down beside her and reached out for her hand, but she drew it away. "What happened?" he asked.

"I wouldn't turn in a story. My editor fired me."

"Why didn't you give him the story?"

"Some good people would have been hurt." Hiller gazed at her and she looked away. "All right, it was stupid. It isn't up to me to protect people. News is news; you've got to be tough."

"I don't think it was stupid."

"And I don't want your sympathy."

"Okay, no sympathy, and no coming with me. You've got to find work."

She looked at him and shook her head. "You've been in space too long, Hiller. I was fired, remember? I've lost tenure. I get to fight with a hundred other people for the public latrine concession or haul trash for two credits a throw. There's a swell room waiting in the bottom levels and I only have to share it with one person. Maybe in a year we'll make enough to go in together on a used autochef so we don't have to eat raw soyeast. Forget it.

I've saved enough to live for two years and that's what I'm going to do. Live."

"It could get messy. I can't watch out for both of us."

Anne shifted; steel flashed in her right hand as her left blurred. She caught Hiller's wrist halfway to his V-coat and laid the knife on his knee.

"I can't watch out for both of us," she mimicked. Hiller felt his cheeks redden.

"Where did you learn that?"

"Alfred Ti-Chen. Two sessions a week for three years. That woman broke my nose, I bought the knife and signed up for the lessons. They've given me a world of confidence."

Hiller stared at the weapon for a moment. It was slim and deadly, with a light taped handle for throwing. He looked up and smiled enigmatically. "May I have my arm back?"

She let go and slipped the knife back into her shirt. "It's really no big deal, you know. Lots of us took self-defense courses. Being a synpape reporter isn't exactly a roof party."

Hiller nodded. "All right; but you will do exactly as I say."

Anne let her breath out. "I will do exactly as you say." He pulled her down on the bed and she raised an eyebrow before giving in. "You didn't tell me there was a catch. . . ."

They didn't catch the hoptercab until nearly two hours later. Hiller sat very still as the craft skimmed just under the dome, the rooftops gliding beneath them. His hand rested on a valise packed with tools known only to the few others like him. After a while Anne began to fidget.

"I suppose you won't be using the lobby again."

Hiller said nothing.

"What if Stanek is home and just didn't answer the phone?"

He sighed. "Then I'll be caught."

"I'm sorry." She put a hand to her mouth and Hiller was forced to smile.

"Please prepare to land," the control box of the cab announced. They looked out and saw the roof of the Brighton Building floating up to meet them.

"It's packed with people," Anne said. "Must be some kind of rally."

As the hopter settled on the cab port, Hiller studied the top floor of its neighbor, Westwood Arms. He wondered again at the risks he was about to take. Conviction for breaking and entering carried a mandatory ten-year term at labor—probably the mines. With his artificial lung he might last seven on the mask-filtered air.

The hopter bumped down. "Insert your credicard now, please," the box intoned, opening the doors only after Hiller complied. A rumble of noise hit them as they climbed down. People were pressing toward the center of the roof where a thin man was exhorting them with a megaphone.

". . . A fully armed Terran battleship, with a complement of one hundred twenty-six human beings. When is it going to end? This makes the seventh—all since our first contact with those *creatures*." Hiller's stomach twisted. Who had it been this time? Spurrier? McLean?

". . . and what does the government do about it?"

"NOTHING!" yelled a dozen voices at once. An angry roar of agreement rose from the crowd and Anne hesitated as Hiller walked ahead to the stairwell.

"Maybe we should get out of here; try it another time."

"No. They'll be a distraction if we need one." He put a hand on her shoulder. "Stay here. If you see me in that doorway waving, call down a cab right away, hold it for five minutes, and then get out." She started to protest, then bit her lip, following his gaze to the glasite fronting the terrace of Stanek's penthouse.

"Right. Be careful."

Hiller nodded and stepped into the stairwell. Five minutes later he had disarmed the fire door alarms at either end of an emergency causeway and was standing in a corridor of the Westwood Arms, nine floors from the top. He boarded the elevator and was about to pry the cover off the controls when he noticed an alarm wire newly soldered around the edge. It would have to be the other way, then. He took the elevator to the last floor below the penthouse. When the doors opened he pushed the button for the next level down and stepped off. As soon as they had closed again he thumbed the call button beside the elevator, braced his feet, and forced the doors open, shearing the inside safety bolt with a loud snap. He hopped onto the top of the cage just as it began to rise again. The shaft was dark and smelled of grease. When the top of the cage pulled level with the penthouse, Hiller palmed the inside catch and stepped into the lobby, opening the valise as he walked over to the door. After a few minutes it yielded and he slipped inside the apartment.

Hiller closed the door and stood for a moment trying to assimilate the room. Later he would comb through his impressions for traces of the man who lived here, but now there was only the room, with its carpet of deep blue grass. Hiller could think of no other term to describe it; it was synthetic, of course, and blue, but otherwise quite like a deep lawn of the last century, its blades curling over his shoe tops. Centered in the middle of the carpet-lawn were two white divans shaped like those of ancient Rome but made of a hard-looking substance which shone like porcelain. Hiller walked over and touched one; it was warm and yielded under his fingers. Between the divans was a low round table cut entirely from crystal. The rest of the furnishings were more conventional: a bar and stools in the corner, a giant trivee gleaming from half of one wall, and metallic curtains drawn across the terrace exposure. From the back of the room an arched hallway led to the ultimate luxury—other rooms. Hiller checked a door behind the bar and found a closet full of expensive V-coats. He smiled grimly; before he was through, they would cost Stanek even more.

The seven-point star was on the wall across from the door. Taking a small egg-shaped instrument from his case, he made a few passes over the emblem, read the atomic weight which registered in a small window, and whistled softly—110.37 Carbon base. It was close to silver—close enough to fool the eye—but it was not silver, and not an alloy either. The star was not from Earth. Hiller drew in a deep breath and let it out slowly; he had linked Stanek to the Proteps.

Pocketing the egg, he moved over to the bar and examined the array of bottles until he found a good set of prints, including a thumb and forefinger of the right hand. He took a transparent strip from the valise, smoothed it over the prints, and sprayed the resulting facsimile with a clear aerosol before dropping it back in the case. Then he went to the closet and left tiny metal slivers from a plastic box in the pocket of every V-coat.

His three most important goals accomplished, Hiller circled the apartment searching behind bedroom drawers, under cushions, and in other favorite hiding places. He turned up nothing and was on his way to the door when he heard the thrum of hopter blades begin and grow steadily louder. Focusing through the terrace curtains, Hiller watched a black executive craft drop from the traffic pattern and swoop toward the roof. It settled in a whirlwind of dust and two figures, one of them hooded and cloaked, began to descend. He recognized Stanek, then felt his blood rush as he caught a glimpse of the face under the cowl. Instinct took over and his hand was on the doorknob before he hesitated. He might never have such a chance again. He slipped instead through the partly open closet door, pushed back through the clothes, and settled himself into the corner as Stanek's key scraped at the lock. The back part of his brain shouted "TRAP" while the front part reviewed the last briefing the Navy had ever given him—an entirely theoretical discussion of the combat capabilities of a Protep.

Six

The terrace door slid open and for the first time Hiller heard nonrecorded Protep speech. It was even more musical than the samples from the programming tapes, soaring and diving through an octave in the course of seconds. Stanek's reply showed amazing mastery of the difficult pitching aspects, but Hiller could not remember enough from the tapes to judge his pronunciation. The voices drew closer; Stanek moved behind the bar and stood with his back to Hiller not four feet away. Ignoring the bottles on top he reached under the bar, withdrew a crystal atomizer, and sprayed mist that sparkled before turning to vapor. The Protep walked up to the bar and Hiller could see the upper half of his body. There had been pictures, of course, but nothing could compare with the actual presence of the creature. He—if indeed it was a male—had thrown back the cowl, baring a forehead that jutted out several inches above the eye sockets and bulged upward in hydrocephalic proportions. The skull was hairless and crisscrossed by veins, dark blue against the cyanic flesh. Because of the forehead ridge above and the cheekbones thrusting out below, the eyes appeared to be sunk deep into the head and Hiller could detect only a hint of bluish-white around the pupils. The alien possessed no external ears and the nose was barely discernible—a slight mound above flaring nostrils. The mouth was a lipless slash; the chin round and small. Proteps were considered humanoid by the biologists but no one had gotten close enough to be certain whether the resemblance exceeded the obvious parody of head and body. Hiller remembered reading that an infant would gaze much longer at a human face than at a randomly arranged pattern of human features. The Protep's face seemed to hold that same attraction, despite or perhaps because of its alienness.

Hiller's foot began to prickle; he mouthed a curse and hoped he would not have to move fast. Stanek pushed a stud under the bar and music started up—a racy symputer variation. At the same time the odor of mint penetrated to the closet. Stanek chattered something and laughed and the alien responded with rasping grunts quite unlike the musical flow of his speech. Hiller nodded and grinned, almost overpowered by the urge to join the laughter. He caught himself in time; bit down on his palm until pain cut through the euphoria. The Protep moved away from the bar revealing a silver embroidered cape over narrow shoulders, and Stanek joined him out of sight. Hiller tried to catch a few words of their conversation; heard his own name spoken in Stanek's baritone with the up-down inflection signifying a question. For a moment the music flowed without interruption; then the alien replied at great length, his voice slowed as if in thought. Hiller shook his head in frustration. If only he had brought along the votaper he could have recorded the conversation and taken it to Porter in linguistics.

The vidphone chimed and Stanek turned down the symputer before answering in English. "Hello, I'm not getting your video." There was a long pause, then: "I see." The music cut off and Stanek said something in a tense voice. Hiller drew the steel leg under him, bracing it against the back wall of the closet. Then the terrace door opened and shut; the hopter stuttered to life, rattling bottles on the bar as it lifted off. Hiller waited until the noise from the craft had faded, then listened for breathing; the rustle of clothes. Satisfied he got up, wincing at the needles in his foot, and walked to the terrace door, looking across at the Brighton.

Gray hopters were settling on the roof, disgorging cadres of black-helmeted riot police. The crowd was beginning to shove against one another as they mobbed the locked exits. Hiller slid the door open a crack and listened to the ugly rumble of their voices. Anne stood where he had left her, by the hopter pad. She was looking up toward the penthouse, one hand hovering over the knife beneath her shirt. He had seen this sort of thing before; in the next few minutes people would die.

Hiller whirled and ran out of the penthouse; fidgeted until the elevator came. Using the fire causeway he had already disarmed, he raced into the hallway of the Brighton. None of the elevators were working and the drop shafts were frozen in midfloor. The roof stairwell was locked, too, and the handle refused to yield.

"Hey! Get away from there."

Hiller turned and watched the black-suited cop bear down on him. "Don't you know there's a riot up top?" the man said. "Now haul ass."

"A friend of mine is up there."

"Get going or I bust you." The cop put a hand on the cudgel at his belt. Hiller hit him with two fingers just under the breastbone and plucked the keys off his belt before the cop had finished sliding down the wall. After six tries he found the right one, pushed through and pounded up the six flights to the roof. Using the key again, he forced the door open against the press of bodies.

"Anne! Over here." The whooping of sirens drowned him out as another wave of hopters settled on the roof. Someone shoved an arm into the doorway and Hiller chopped at it.

"Jad!"

Hiller opened the door another few inches and kicked out with the steel foot clearing a space. His view was obstructed when someone crashed against the opening and crumpled down spitting blood. He caught a glimpse of knife handle sticking out below the man's shoulder, then saw a flash of yellow, the color of Anne's shirt. Reaching out, he grabbed for her arm and pulled her through the doorway, letting it slam under the thrusting bodies. He twisted the key and looked her up and down. A trickle of blood ran down her forehead and a purplish bruise was forming under her right eye, but she managed a weak smile.

"Next time I get to do the dangerous stuff."

Hiller handed her a glass of whiskey as full as his own and sat next to her on the bed.

"That's a nasty mouse." He probed gently under her eye. She winced and brushed his hand away. After gazing fondly around the apartment she sighed and laid back, propping the drink on her chest.

"It was a bad one, Jad—the worst I've seen. Everyone's in a lather about the ship. For twenty years the government's been giving them a line about new worlds where the air is fresh and food grows on trees. Just when it looks like we've got the ships to pull it off, they start popping out of existence. The official explanation this time is malfunction of the Opperman drives—the ship accidently got suspended in hyperspace—but those people on the roof weren't buying it."

"How about you?" he asked.

"I don't know." She tried to sip her drink, coughed and sat up. "God knows I've run out as many Protep theories as anyone, but maybe we're all just looking for scapegoats. I mean, theoretically the Oppermans really could be malfunctioning. We only developed them in the past six or seven years and no one seems sure just how they work. Besides, isn't that what made your ship blow up?"

Hiller stared through her until she reached up and tapped his chest.

"Uh—sorry. Yes, the Oppermans definitely exploded. The question is, why?" He spoke slowly, his eyes still distant. "The rescue ship *Littlejohn* swept up the space debris of the *Trojan* and navy labs have been sifting through them ever since. They also took aboard an arm and leg belonging to a boy named Edwards, most of a Russian engineer too tough to be blown apart, and the head . . ."

"Jad, stop it."

He nodded and drained his glass. "But there was something they didn't find. They didn't find so much as a fingernail of York, my signal officer."

"But couldn't he have just been . . ."

"Blown into pieces too small to find? I suppose so." He hesitated. "There's something I didn't tell you—something I remembered when I first saw Stanek's star emblem through the keyhole." He told her about the Protep ship that had appeared on his viewscreen before the explosion. "Suppose for a minute that York was connected with the Proteps—like Stanek. He might have been able to sabotage the engines and then escape through a service lock to be picked up by the ship."

She gripped his arm. "Have you told this—about the ship—to Naval Intelligence?"

"No."

"Why not?"

He got up and began to pace. "Because I'm not sure. I had a lot of dreams while I was in the hospital; some of them were pretty real. Maybe I'm just remembering a dream." He poured another whiskey, looked at it, and then tipped it back into the bottle, spilling some on his hands. He picked up a smooth blue stone from the collection on a wall shelf and examined it critically. "At least I'm not dreaming about Stanek," he said at last. "He is connected with the Proteps."

"Yes, but you still have no proof that he's Pavel."

"The proof is in the valise," he said. "In another day we'll know for sure."

"What if he's not Pavel," Anne persisted. "Will you let it go, then?"

Hiller studied her before answering. "No. If he's not Martin Pavel then I can forget the business about his arm and his youngness; but there's still the matter of his association with the Proteps. I didn't just lose half my body out there, I lost my ship. I want to know why Stanek speaks better Protep than the top five linguists in the world. I want to know why he's their golden-haired boy when they won't let our official emissaries close to them. I want to know what he does for them and why. Maybe it won't lead me any closer to why the *Trojan* blew up under me, but maybe it will."

"Isn't this a matter for your former colleagues?" she asked gently.

"Why? They never tell me things any more." He smiled with everything but his eyes, pulled a suitcase from under the bed, and began to pack.

She got up and helped.

Seven

After touring the lot of rental hopters at the cross-country pads just outdome, Hiller selected an old two-seater equipped with luggage hold and survival kit. He chose it over the newer models because of its obsolete interlock system, protected only by a metal plate. The Protep embassy was a short hop away and Hiller had barely tested the controls before they were descending through the haze locked on a holding pattern from the control tower. The smog thinned and the dome of the embassy reached up at them, flanked by the spire of the tower. Under the center of the dome, the chancery—a monolith of yellow-white stone unmarred by windows—commanded its moat of grass. The lawn was blue-green and Hiller could see the mist of sprinklers as they drew closer. The use of water for such luxury had drawn fire from the populist synpapes; Hiller found it merely ironic that the biggest lawn on Earth was maintained by aliens. On the outer fringe of the grass under the curvature of the dome, sat smaller buildings of the same quarried stone as the chancery. Three planetfall class cruisers currently occupied the pads in back of the dome, their flanks skirted by staff hopters and service trucks.

"Tower to approaching hopter, please identify yourself." Anne jumped and Hiller glanced at the radio; it was dead—there had been no warning crackle of static. He gave their names and the purpose of their visit and, to his surprise, was immediately given a landing beam. Four Proteps wearing tight yellow suits and breathing masks waited beside the pad as the hopter touched down.

"You wish to see the ambassador?" one of them asked after Hiller and Anne had adjusted their own masks and stepped down.

"That's right. . . ." Hiller swallowed the arguments he had prepared as the alien simply nodded and motioned for them to follow him. A guard fell in on either side and behind as the spokesman led them through the airlock and halted before an iron gate backed by the distortion of a force field. They shed their masks and the leader turned to Hiller.

"It will be necessary to touch you," he said with a remote expression. Hiller nodded, permitting the alien to search him with deft fingers while another did the same to Anne. He admired their thoroughness; the scanners, whose presence was revealed by a vibration in his artificial tooth, might miss weapons like a garrote or plastic explosives. The alien straightened and faced the gate. It swung open and the force field flickered off, letting out the smell of mown grass. Hiller expanded his lungs once and again, more deeply. So this was what it had been like—the air of the last century, with its infusion of water; its subtle blend of plant gases. The light seemed bright and Hiller looked up at the underside of the dome. At strategic points, white globes supplemented the feeble sunlight, making the mist sparkle and dropping shadows at their feet. There were no sidewalks and the lawn felt good under Hiller's shoes after the hard planes of the city. A few Proteps in red robes passed them as they crossed to the chancery, but none returned Hiller's gaze. He toyed with the idea that Proteps lacked a curiosity drive, then cleared his mind as they entered the building, letting the cool of the hallway and the echo of their steps occupy his attention. They stopped in front of a door.

"The female will wait outside," said the Protep who had done all the talking. Anne started to protest but Hiller put a hand on her arm and she fell silent. The door opened.

Eight

Hiller found himself in a large windowless room that nevertheless seemed to be flooded with sunlight like the brilliant white rays of Epsilon Eridani. There was no desk or file, nor anything which could pass for them; only two divans made of plush red material and a crystal table between them like the setup in Stanek's apartment.

The largest Protep Hiller had ever seen was reclining on one of the couches. His head was heavily veined and a luxurious gold cape covered shoulders which were broad for one of his race. His hands, too, were thick and strong-looking in contrast to other aliens Hiller had seen.

"I am Kotyro, representative to this planet of his serenity, Lord Cvirko. You will be seated and partake of the wine of greeting." Hiller blinked as a goblet filled with amber liquid appeared on the table. The ambassador drank deeply, then held out the cup to Hiller. Hiller stretched awkwardly on his side in imitation of Kotyro and accepted the goblet, passing the snooper in his ring over it before drinking. The wine had a peculiar sharp fragrance and tasted delicious.

"I am honored to greet you," Hiller said, putting the cup back on the table.

"What is it that you want, Captain?"

"There is a man named Stanek—an old acquaintance. He is the friend of a Protep who, I assume, is associated with the embassy. I would like to explore the nature of this relationship."

The ambassador studied him for a moment. "You speak with a directness quite uncharacteristic of your species," he said at last. "I find it quite refreshing." Hiller inclined his head at the compliment. "I trust that you will not be offended, then," the alien continued, "when I tell you that you have spoken partly in error. All Proteps on your planet are indeed associated with the embassy. So, in fact, is Mr. Stanek. However, it is quite inconceivable that the two should be friends."

"Why do you say that?"

"Mr. Hiller, we have known your species far too short a time to permit any such relationship to develop. I perceive from my limited study of humans that friendships may be formed quickly between individuals. This is quite impossible among my people."

Hiller frowned. "Mr. Ambassador, we may simply be differing in our use of the term friendship. I meant only that the Protep was in Stanek's apartment—the two were laughing, talking—in your language I might add—and listening to music together. To me, friendship does not appear too strong a word to describe such behavior."

"It is as I have told you. You may believe as you like—a practice I have encountered, by the way, in a number of your species. I simply wished to spare you continued misunderstanding."

Hiller digested the point. If Proteps could indeed form friendships only very slowly, it helped explain why they had forbidden access to their own planet despite many friendly overtures from Earth. Perhaps what had been interpreted as hostility was merely innate caution. Of course, it all depended on whether Kotyro was being candid.

"You said that Stanek is associated with your embassy."

"That is correct. We have hired him to act in a liaison capacity in certain areas. For example, he advises us on matters of human custom and interpretation, so that our dealings with your species may proceed more smoothly. That, of course, is why he has been taught our language."

"An honor which has not yet officially been conferred on any human other than Stanek," Hiller reminded him. "So far you have forced us to rely on a patchwork of those words and expressions our linguists can identify through context."

Kotyro's eyes were enigmatic pools of shadow. "Mr. Hiller, a language is the soul of those who speak it—the key to understanding the most intimate detail of their thoughts. We must be quite certain of your soul before we reveal our own."

"My people have a different philosophy," Hiller countered. "It's called mutual trust."

The alien appeared amused. "Please, Mr. Hiller. We are not a naïve people. Even in your own history mutual trust has seldom prevailed in the absence of equal power and position. The trust you speak of is an epiphenomenon of a balanced bargaining position—one which your species hardly occupies with respect to ours."

Hiller flushed. Why had he let the discussion be continually drawn to generalities when it was Stanek who concerned him? "What if Stanek comes to our linguists and teaches them what you have taught him?"

"That is quite impossible. The technique by which he learned our language ensures that he may not pass his knowledge to another."

Hiller wondered how such a thing might be done. Strong posthypnotic suggestion? Conditioning? He tried to marshal his thoughts. The alien seemed to have done what, beneath the crust of his objectivity, he had most feared—destroyed the suspicious appearance of Stanek's association with the Proteps. Still, the issue of whether Stanek was Pavel remained unresolved.

"Just how do you pay Mr. Stanek for his work?" Hiller asked.

"Why with your credits, of course. We obtain such of your money as we require for such purposes through the exchange of certain metals valued by your government. Why do you ask?"

Hiller took another sip of the wine while weighing his next words. He had nothing to lose, he decided, by telling Kotyro of the climbing accident twenty-five years before. If he did not, the conversation could proceed no further. When he had finished his account the ambassador made a few of the same rasping sounds Hiller remembered from the Protep in Stanek's apartment. The alien steepled his hands toward the floor as he laughed—if, indeed, that was what he was doing.

"You give us too much credit, Mr. Hiller," he said finally. "Alas, we could not restore one of our own limbs, nor preserve our youth, let alone do so for one of your species."

Hiller started to get up, feeling a sudden dizziness. He looked at the wine goblet as the alien raised a hand. "But I fear I have been tactless," Kotyro said. "Please do not be offended by my amusement. I see now why you are so interested in Mr. Stanek."

Hiller sank down again. "What do you mean?"

"Tell me, were you not curious that I, the ambassador, should immediately agree to meet with a person of your nonofficial status?"

"Yes," Hiller admitted.

"It is because you are a person who particularly interests us."

"I don't understand."

"Here at the embassy it is daily procedure to digest the information recorded in your major synpapes. An article of special significance to us appeared in most of them approximately eleven months ago." Hiller felt his heart quicken. "I refer, of course, to the news of the loss of your ship."

"Why should that interest you?"

"Because we recorded an explosion 195 secarts—roughly equal to 270 of your miles—off our planet just before those articles were printed. We subsequently read of your remarkable survival from this treacherous spy mission—you lost an arm, I believe, along with certain other parts of your body . . ."

"It's true, then; I did see one of your ships. . . ." Hiller realized his mistake at once. He could not have blundered so badly—unless . . . He held the glass up in mock salute and then poured the contents on the floor while the alien watched impassively.

"It appears that I have been a fool."

"You should feel no shame that I outwitted you," Kotyro said matter-of-factly. "Your downfall came merely from knowing less of me than I know of you. You could hardly have refused to drink the wine, especially since I drank before you. The chemical is very mild and unknown to your drug detectors; I, of course, am not susceptible, due to physiological differences I fear you will have to content yourself with guessing at."

"You have recorded everything?"

"Of course."

"What will you do with it?"

"Perhaps nothing. It depends on whether any advantage may be gained in the future by proving that an Earth spy ship tried to violate our territorial space. It could become an embarrassment to your government under the right circumstances. As to the ship you claim to have seen, I said nothing of any ship. Our planetary observation posts were entirely adequate to unmask the clumsy approach of your ship."

Hill felt a sharp burning in his ears. The alien had maneuvered him as easily as a child, turning the conversation in the directions he liked almost at will. "Do you deny the presence of one of your vessels just before the *Trojan* exploded?"

"My dear Captain Hiller, you disappoint me. Surely I need not remind a man of your sophistication that anything I might admit or deny must be of little consequence. The votaper, after all, is mine. I'm sure you're aware that I have told you only what I wish you to believe; nor am I foolish enough to expect that you will believe anything I have said. I am content merely to have told you nothing."

Hiller raised an eyebrow. "Your deviousness is a fact worth knowing."

Kotyro spread his hands. "Hopefully it will not be a matter to concern you again." Kotyro stood in a fluid motion and Hiller got up too, finding himself no longer dizzy. "I have no wish to be cruel," the ambassador said. "I know the penalty your government would impose on you should it become necessary for us to reveal your indiscretion. Let us hope that it does not become necessary."

"I find it interesting that you should want to threaten me," Hiller said.

"Threaten you?" The alien's face was a mask. "You have misunderstood me. I merely want to assure you that I will NOT use your damaging admission without good cause. In any case, what reason could I possibly have for threatening you? You are hardly in a position to do me harm."

"Perhaps; perhaps not," Hiller said. "My government might be quite interested to learn certain things about another of your human employees—a man called York."

The alien looked at him for what seemed a bit too long before responding. "We have only a few humans working for us and none of them is called York."

"If you say so. I thought you might like to hear a theory I have about York, but I can see that you're not interested."

"Good-by, Mr. Hiller. It might be wise of you to put yourself out of reach of your former employers."

"Thanks for the advice, Mr. Ambassador; next time let's skip the refreshments." Hiller walked to the door and it slid back in front of him. He turned after stepping through and met the Protep's gaze until the door slid shut. Anne was waiting where he had left her, still in the company of the four guards. She said nothing until they had been ushered back aboard their hopter and were airborne on a Richmond beam. Then she turned in her seat.

"Well?"

"I may have salvaged a draw," Hiller said. He told her what had happened.

"M-m-m; not good," she said when he'd finished. "They could execute you under the Secrets Act."

"I don't think Kotyro really intends to use it," Hiller said. "It could be embarrassing but no more. Both sides clearly knew already that we violated Protep air space on a spy mission. No, Kotyro was bending over backward to keep me from taking it as a personal threat, but he wants it hanging over my head, in case I start making trouble. I find it very encouraging."

The desolate sand mounds swept beneath them, barely visible through the yellow haze as the hopter climbed on its beam to 2,500 feet. Anne settled back in her seat with a resigned expression. "Kotyro can get you canceled and you find it encouraging."

"It means I'm on the right track," Hiller said. "I think I scored with my gambit on York, and there is definitely something about

Stanek that the ambassador doesn't want me to know. He brought out the threat before I even mentioned York."

Anne nodded. "Okay. What do we do next?"

Hiller studied the screens on the instrument panel before responding. "Feel like a trip to Canada?" he asked finally.

"Canada? Why did you get us a Richmond beam?"

Hiller looked at his rear screen again. "Because before we commit ourselves I'd like to find out who is following us and why."

Nine

Hiller requested a course change, just to be sure, and the other craft followed suit. It was too far back to be seen and showed only as a small blip holding a constant position near the perimeter of the rear screen.

"Who could it be?" Anne asked.

"He's a professional, whoever he is," Hiller said. "He's keeping a thousand feet back and to port, right in the train of our turbulence where I might mistake him for a drive echo." Hiller put the hopter on auto and climbed back into the storage section, retrieving his valise.

"What are you doing?"

"I'm going to force things a bit—find out if our friend is private or official." He took out some tools and removed the cover on the controls, finding the computer interlock.

"Hey, isn't that dangerous?"

"And illegal," Hiller admitted, "but so is slugging a policeman, breaking and entering, and violating the Official Secrets Act. Maybe our luck will hold."

Anne peered anxiously into the yellow soup surrounding the hopter. "What if we ram somebody?"

"That's what viewscreens are for. I've overridden these things a few times and my reflexes are still pretty good. Besides, outdome traffic never amounts to much on the hopter levels. All the commercial stuff is higher up." He finished bypassing the interlock and scrambled back to his seat as the craft broke away from the beam and began to buck. He brought it under control and then sent it into a dive, which pinned them against their seats.

"Jar-RED!"

"Hang on and watch the rear screen," Hiller said.

"Craft 8601H, this is CompCentral." The flat mechanical voice filled the hopter. "You have lost course contact. Activate emergency landing program at once; repeat, activate ELP at once. Your craft will be located and assistance will be sent." The message repeated itself. They plunged downward through the haze until the altimeter read five hundred feet and the sandy hillocks leaped up below them.

"It's gone," Anne said. "No, wait . . . it's back."

"That takes care of that," Hiller said grimly. "We've got something special on our tail. Even if the other guy knew how to break the interlock it would take him longer than that to react—unless he's not on interlock. Let's see what he's made of." Hiller jacked the controls around; the craft swung 180 degrees and hurtled down on the now approaching hopter.

"Jad, there's another blip." His eyes darted to the screen and he grunted in irritation.

"They're flanking us." A large blue shape popped out of the haze and flashed by. Hiller caught a glimpse of a strained face in the bubble above the white block lettering on the nose of the craft.

"PLANESEC," he muttered. At the same instant a voice crackled in the air-to-air speakers.

"This is Planetary Security. Put it down, Hiller. Put it down or we fire." The voice sounded tense; vaguely familiar.

Hiller thumbed the switch under his own mike. "What kind of talk is that?"

"Just pull the plug," the voice snapped.

Hiller reached over and activated the ELP. The hopter lost speed and began to settle as the two blips, now on the forward screen, arced around and bore back toward him in a pincer movement.

Anne looked at him in surprise. "You're giving up?"

"I'll let them have my ante this time," Hiller said. "I don't like betting that those two wouldn't roast us."

The ground rushed up at them, then slowed in the last seconds as the stabilizers cut in and lowered them with a gentle bump. The rotor died and Hiller reached up above him, pulling down his mask. "Better slip into yours, too," he said. "They'll want us outside."

The other two craft landed on either side and three men climbed down from one of them. "They are nervous," Hiller said. "Those aren't needlers they're pointing at us."

"So be nice to them," Anne said, eying the blasters.

"Get your ass out of there, Hiller," a voice said on the ATA. "And bring the fem with you." Hiller looked across to the hopter which still held its crew. A granite face stared at him through the tinted plastite. He shrugged and climbed down, with Anne right behind him. The sand felt hot against his foot and he shifted his weight to the steel leg.

"Just keep your distance," one of the men on the ground warned. "I know all about your special options." The man who spoke was short and compact; dressed like the others in a dusty blue jump suit. His eyes were hidden behind a sun shield that fit down over his mask, but his bald head was bare and had already begun to glisten in the heat. He motioned with his blaster. "Search them."

"Sure thing, Lieutenant." The man on Hiller's left started forward eagerly, his eyes fixed on Anne.

"A word of caution, friend. . . ." Hiller began.

"Shaddap." The man moved around behind Anne and slid his hands under her arms, letting his fingers stray forward. Her heel lashed up behind as she grabbed his hair and jackknifed at the waist, using her hip and one leg as a lever. The man yelled and hurtled over her shoulder, landing heavily on his back. The bald man's gun arm stiffened toward Anne, but she stood quietly, her hands raised. The other man snickered and then broke off at a sharp glance from the lieutenant.

"All you had to do was ask," Anne said sweetly. She removed the knife slowly and dropped it on the sand. The man in front of her groaned and staggered up. He took a step toward her and the lieutenant snorted.

"Forget it. Just check Hiller and get back over here."

"I don't like guns," Hiller said as the man patted him down sullenly. "They mess up the tailoring."

"All right," the lieutenant said when his man had rejoined him. "Just what do you two think you're doing?" Suddenly Hiller recognized the voice; connected it with the bald stocky figure.

"So you've gone over to PLANESEC, eh, Pierce?" he said. "The Navy get tired of your face too?"

"Pretty sharp. I didn't think you'd remember me. As a matter of fact, I got a better offer from Planetary Security."

"But now you have to work with goons," Hiller pointed out. Pierce glanced to either side and nodded glumly. "They're not all as bad as these two. Answer my question, Hiller."

"We were planning a little trip."

"Where to?"

"I'd rather not say. At least not until I find out why you care."

Pierce looked up at the sky and Hiller could imagine the pained expression beneath the mask. "C'mon, we're both professionals; can't we talk straight and skip the fencing?" Hiller shrugged and waited. "All right," Pierce said in resignation. "You've been following a man named Stanek—a guy who works at the Protep embassy. You let yourself into his apartment and left in kind of a hurry. Then you showed up at the embassy. We want to know why."

"And I'm still wondering why you care."

"You want me to burn him a little, Lootenant?" asked the man who had laughed.

"Shut up, Kuntz. We care because, whatever your interests are in Stanek, we have a few of our own. We'd like it very much if some yoo-hoo didn't go blundering around just now and giving him the scare."

"That's better," Hiller said. "Maybe we can do business. I'm interested in Stanek because he looks like a man I knew once—a man who owes me money."

"Uh huh; and I'm Captain Fury's virgin sister. You're not doing your part, Hiller."

"Will it help if I promise to keep clear of Stanek?"

"Oh, you're going to do that anyway. Because if you don't, I'm going to put you away, purple heart and sunbursts or no. I want to know why."

"Look, Eddie, I'd like to help you; but in the first place you wouldn't believe me and in the second, it doesn't matter anyway. It was something personal and I cleared things up at the embassy."

"Was?"

"You have my promise that Anne and I are on our way to a vacation in Canada. You can even follow us if you want." Hiller paused. "By the way, why are you after Stanek?"

"Hiller, you haven't earned the time of day from me; but I like one thing you said. I think a nice vacation in Canada would be good for you right now. As a matter of fact some of the goons here are going to tag along at a discreet distance and see that you have a good time. For old time's sake I'll pass up putting the screws on you—you were always square with me when I was an ensign. But there's two things I want to say before you go." Pierce held up two pudgy fingers. "One, stay away from Stanek. He's worse than a communicable social disease right now. Two, watch yourself. It's not a good idea for a man with your background and knowledge to be talking with Proteps. If it happens again, your name will go right under Stanek's on my exclusive little list. Clear?"

"Perfectly."

"Good. Then you can hoist back aboard your hopter. One other thing; I recommend you stay on interlock. That way my boys won't get itchy to try out one of their heat-seekers. They've been tuning them to your hull signal while we talked."

"Naturally."

"Have fun in Canada," Pierce said, glancing at Anne. Then he climbed aboard his hopter, followed by the other two, and both craft lifted away and quickly disappeared into the haze. The thrumming of one of them held at a fixed point above them until they were back inside the soundproof bubble of their own hopter; the green blip stayed on their screens all the way to Calgary.

After securing the hopter at a guarded rental pad outside the citydome, Hiller and Anne entered through a lock and transferred their bags to a city hoptercab. Hiller looked over the packed rooftops with interest as the cab carried them to the Hawthorne Hotel, next to Mercy Hospital. Calgary had been forced to dome over in the year 2027—years after most of the cities—when the sulfur oxides alone hit an average of two parts per million and thousands of citizens had died. Occasionally with exactly proper conditions it was still possible to go outdome without a mask, but few ever tried it. In the twenty-five years since he'd last seen Calgary, its few remaining squares of ground had sprouted their inevitable steel towers to inch upward like bars on a population graph. The sky outside the dome was surprisingly clear, and Hiller thought he could make out the shadowy peaks of the Rockies, which loomed only a few miles outdome. There was no obvious sign of the PLANESEC agents Pierce had sent to tail him, but Hiller knew they were there. He would flush them when the time came.

After settling in the cramped room on the sixty-seventh, with its fold-down double bed and tiny bathroom, Hiller installed a small powerlock of his own on the door and took Anne down to the restaurant.

"When are you going to do what you came for?" she asked, after they had settled in a booth with red cushions and high synthoak backs.

"Just as soon as we've ordered drinks," Hiller told her. She just looked at him. He pushed the button in the table and called for a scotch and a bourbon; then he studied the menu on the wall for a moment. "I recommend the Irish stew," he said as he got up.

"Where are you going?"

"To the men's room. Enjoy your dinner." He slid the hotel room key across to her under a napkin and walked away as she opened and then closed her mouth. The restrooms were at the rear, opening off a small hallway that led to the kitchen. Without looking back at the crowd of diners, Hiller pulled the door open, stepped behind it, and then slipped instead through the double doors into the kitchen. A waiter bustled over immediately.

"Sir, guests are not permitted in the kitchen."

"Would you kindly show me to your service lift," Hiller said, opening his wallet. The waiter looked around quickly and took his arm, ushering him past steaming autochefs to the back of the kitchen. Hiller gave him a five-credit note and stepped into the elevator. It dropped three stories and then opened onto an underground loading bay next to the freight tubes. He found a stairway to street level and minutes later the antiseptic odor of the hospital scrubbed the lingering smell of soyeast from his nostrils.

He examined the lobby, quickly settling on an elderly receptionist sitting at a desk in the corner. She wore thick glasses and was peering at a detective magazine held inches from her face. As he walked up she let it drop quickly to a more normal reading distance. Hiller smiled inwardly and brought out his I.D., holding it up for her to see.

"I'm Miller from the P.A.'s office," he said. "I've come to look at the old records." She squinted at the I.D. but did not move closer.

"Which records?" she said in a thin whiny voice.

"From twenty-five years ago. Didn't they call you?"

"They never tell me anything," she complained. "Did you say twenty-five years ago? Listen, mister, stuff that far back is still waiting to be brought over to the microfilm system."

"I'm aware of that," Hiller said, concealing his surprise. "Just take me to the records, will you? The administrator said you'd co-operate fully."

"Well, I don't care what he said, I'm not going down in that basement," the old woman announced. "One of the nurses got raped down there just last month and they don't pay me to take that kind of chance." She fumbled in the desk and brought out a tagged key. "It's Room 104; you can help yourself." Hiller picked up the key.

"This is 107," he said. She snatched it back and sorted through the drawer more carefully until she found the right key.

"If you're from the P.A.'s office maybe you can do something about the crime in this hospital instead of crawling around in a bunch of dusty old records," she said as she slid it across to him. Hiller accepted the key with a properly chastened look and walked to the stairwell, hurrying only after the door had swung shut behind him.

There were ten flights leading down into the deepest level—the 100's—which was the maximum depth permitted by the water table under Calgary. Hiller entered the bottom corridor and wrinkled his nose against the dank musty smell. The lights were spaced far apart and the floor was damp concrete. He ducked under the network of pipes which festooned the ceiling and made his way to the records room.

There was a single light in the middle of the ceiling; scuttling noises greeted him as he turned it on. Rusted metal files lined the walls and anchored a tangle of cobwebs stretching into the dark corners of the room. Hiller found the file marked 2050 and was about to open the drawer labeled Ma-Pe when he noticed something. It wasn't much—just a clean spot the size of a finger tip, surrounded on the handle of the drawer by caked dust. Hiller examined some of the other drawers but their coating of dust was undisturbed. He checked the ceiling to make sure that dripping water hadn't caused the spot, then pulled the drawer open. He found Pavel's card after only a minute and pocketed it, along with several others on either side of it. Then he switched off the light and returned to the lobby, leaving the key with the receptionist and making his way through an alley back to the hotel. A long-faced man in a plaid V-coat straightened against a pillar as Hiller entered the Hawthorne's lobby. The man quickly slouched again, but not before Hiller had stored a mental copy of him.

Anne was pacing in their room when he let himself in with the duplicate. She came over. "The stew was passable; how was your night?"

"We'll know in a minute." Hiller pulled the cards from his pocket and moved over to the bed, opening his valise and taking out several items. First he laid the plastic strip with Stanek's prints beside the ones on Pavel's admission card and studied them both. Then, frowning, he took a small knife and pried loose Pavel's photograph and one from another card, depositing a drop of pink solution on the dried paste which remained on the cards. The solution turned clear on the card of the stranger but remained pink on Pavel's card. He stared at the two cards for a long time.

"Damn it, Jad, are they or aren't they Stanek's?"

"Oh, they're different. But only because somebody switched Pavel's picture to one of the old blank cards at the back of the file and redid everything, substituting phony prints." He held up the bottle with the pink solution. "Up until a few years ago one of the ingredients of paste was starch," he explained; "stuff that turns this phenolphthalein solution clear. Because of shortages, newer varieties of paste haven't contained starch for over ten years—that's why the solution on Pavel's card stayed pink."

"So the prints have been switched," she said. "That really rips it."

"As far as proving anything goes," Hiller agreed. "But maybe what it tells us is more valuable than proof of something I already believe. They took a gamble. If I had compared the prints and let it go at that, they would have won. This way . . ." Hiller broke off and stared at a small metal box which had fallen out of his valise when he removed the other things. A tiny red light was pulsing rapidly in one corner of it. Anne walked over, started to touch it, and then drew her finger back uncertainly.

"What is it? What does the light mean?"

Hiller picked it up, cradling it in one hand. "It means," he said slowly, "that Martin Stanek is here—in Calgary."

Ten

Anne stared at the box. "It's some sort of . . . ?"

"It's a tracking monitor," Hiller said. "When I was in Stanek's apartment I put tracers in his coats. Just before we left for the embassy I checked the monitor and his blip was still there, just as you'd expect."

"What's the range?"

"About ten miles."

"Then he's followed us here."

"Not necessarily. Maybe we followed him."

Anne nodded slowly. "You mean he came here and changed the prints?"

"It makes sense. It's unlikely he'd be here at all, unless he really is Pavel and got worried that I'd be digging up the old trail." The flasher began to slow a bit; Hiller gathered up the things on the bed and crammed them into the valise. "Get your stuff together," he said. "Stanek's moving away from us at walking speed toward the north edge of town—the hopter pads." He moved to the door.

"Where are you going?"

"One of Pierce's boys is lounging in the lobby," he explained. "He'd be crushed if we left without saying good-by."

Anne tried to read his expression. "I have a feeling he's going to be crushed when you do say good-by."

"Not unless he gets unpleasant." The metal fingers flexed. "It won't do to have Pierce tailing through us to Stanek; give me five minutes, then get a bellhop to help you with the luggage. I'll meet you at the pads as soon as possible." Hiller thrust his I.D. card into the door slot, which hummed and spat out a receipt for three hours' occupancy. He handed the slip to Anne along with the monitor.

"What if Stanek takes off before you get to the pads?"

"Try to follow him if he goes commercial, and call me at the Hawthorne when you get a chance."

She nodded. Hiller shut the door and went down to the lobby. The horse-faced man had left his spot by the pillar and had changed out of the plaid V-coat, but Hiller spotted him right away, sitting on one of the settees across from the door. This time the man did not look at him but rubbed his jaw with one big-knuckled hand, his lips moving slightly. Hiller smiled; PLANESEC was still using the outmoded whisper rings. They always were behind the trade in everything but melodrama, he reflected as he strolled across the faded carpet to the door. The fellow on the settee had no doubt signaled a roof lookout that Hiller was leaving from the lobby; it was the usual three-man stakeout, with the third party posted at the hopter pads. Hiller wondered if they knew Stanek was also in town; something—perhaps an instinctive assessment of the man—made him doubt it.

He stepped out into dry heat, a sign that the city's circulation plant had been poorly installed by American profiteers. The gaps between buildings were wider and more well-traveled than the ones in Washington, and the buildings were lower, letting in light even as the sun settled behind the Rockies. Glare strips began to supplement the failing sunlight and Hiller looked ahead for a narrow unlit alley as he pushed through the tide of people. He knew without looking back that horse-face was following him; he imagined the sweat on the man's forehead; the eyes straining. Hiller felt his stomach twist at the thought that his own quarry might be slipping away while he tried to shake Pierce's men.

He saw a crease between buildings and swerved into it, stopping in the darkness. Backing against one wall, he braced his feet against the other and ignored the painful scrape of brick along his back as he thrust upward to a height of ten feet. He waited, controlling his breathing. The stench of rotted yeast-skim filled the alley and a cobweb brushed against his face as he listened to the flow of the crowd outside. A wave of protest followed horse-face's rude passage forward and Hiller was ready when the man burst into the alley beneath him. He kicked downward connecting with the top of the skull and dropped onto the man's legs as he pitched forward, holding back a rabbit punch when he saw that horse-face was already out cold. He rolled the man over to get his face out of some garbage, turned, and froze. The alley mouth was nearly filled by a silhouette; Hiller's mind flashed back to the square-visored face in the PLANESEC hopter.

"Now that wasn't nice at all," the shadow drawled. "Hector ain't going to thank you when he wakes up."

"Shouldn't you be on the hotel roof in case I double back, get the woman, and take off in a cab?" Hiller asked.

"Naw. Pierce didn't give us no orders about the fem; only you, and you're here, ain't you?" The man stepped forward, slapping one ham fist into the other palm. Hiller thought about running; decided there wasn't time for a chase if he meant to keep on Stanek's trail.

"How much do they pay you at PLANESEC?" he asked. The other man chuckled. Hiller dilated the pupil of his right eye and set it at the edge of the body-heat frequencies, giving himself a red outline to aim at. The man lunged and Hiller stabbed at his jaw, drawing only a grunt. A haymaker crashed against the side of his head; the giant grabbed his V-coat and was launching another roundhouse when Hiller managed to bring a knee into his groin. He bellowed and doubled over, exposing the base of his neck. Hiller's eyes swam; in slow motion he chopped again and again at the offered target. Incredibly, the giant straightened and clutched at Hiller before sagging against the wall. Hiller stepped around him and stumbled out of the alley, his head still ringing.

He had no memory of getting to a roof and hailing a cab; and his head was only a little clearer when he bought a mask from a vending machine, cycled through the hopter-pad lock, and shuffled to the edge of the lighted pad area. Then pain started up over one ear and cleared his head like a tonic. He scanned the pads; saw Anne standing by their hopter and a man in a blue jump suit peering at her from behind a black hopter five pads away. As Hiller watched, the man held a receiver up to his ear, glared at it, and shook it. Keeping to the darkness outside the pads, Hiller circled behind the man, and in a minute it was over.

Anne met him as soon as she saw him coming and held out the monitor.

"Where's Stanek?" he asked.

"He took off about a minute ago. In another few seconds I'd have had to follow him alone. What took you so long?" Her eyes shifted to the knot that was swelling on the side of Hiller's head and she winced. He climbed into the hopter and thumbed the starter as she carded the rental payment and hopped up beside him. The metal rings holding their landing struts popped open, their seats pressed upward, and the light thinned and fell away, shrinking to a dot below them as they spiraled into a holding pattern.

Hiller pulled off his mask; studied the monitor and ship screen. "I think that's him," he said after a moment, pointing to one of three blips on the screen. "The bearing is right and so is the speed. Looks like a commercial beam, too, at that altitude." Relief showed on his face. If Stanek stayed on the commercial routes they could follow him without arousing suspicion. Hiller flipped the CompCentral switch and requested an easterly beam, watching his screens until he was satisfied that their course was parallel to Stanek's. Then he settled back against the webfoam and rubbed his eyes. Blackness engulfed the bubble of their hopter and the green lights of the instrument panel moved in and out of focus. Anne eyed him.

"You need rest," she said.

He nodded; reached for the hopter's medikit and then changed his mind. Painkillers would help him sleep but they would also gum up his thinking and reflexes. "We'll sleep in shifts," he said. "One of us has to keep an eye on the monitor.

We don't know where Stanek's beam is coming down, or even if he'll stay on beam. Something tells me he knows how to break interlock without frying himself."

They followed Stanek away from the sun for twenty-one hours, including a fuel stop and an eight-hour layover in southern Manitoba, before Hiller's prediction was confirmed. Both craft were about a hundred miles north of the Michinois border and night was falling again when Anne shook him awake. The pain in his head had subsided to a dull ache.

"Jad, he's broken off and is heading south."

Hiller studied the blip that had curved away and begun to grow faint. "It's dropping out of range—he's low enough to follow on monitor without us showing up on his screens." He scrambled to the control box and got them off beam, ignoring the recorded warning from CompCentral. They followed Stanek at a safe distance while his hopter crossed the border and curved toward the coast of Lake Michigan. The flashing light on the monitor began suddenly to quicken.

"He's landed," Hiller said, jumping to the jury-rigged controls. He brought the craft down a few miles from Stanek between two hillocks of sand. They put on their masks and hopped down. After studying the monitor in the glow of a pen light, Hiller started off at a brisk pace, Anne following. They walked in silence for a while. The air was hot and damp and the moon a ghost in the haze about them. Hiller's shirt clung to his back and mosquitoes swarmed around them, biting at their hands and necks. Hiller tried walking without the beam but gave up after Anne stumbled twice.

"Take it easy," she whispered. "Only one of us can see in the dark. How much further?" Hiller checked the monitor, whose light had become a continuous blur.

"We must be almost on top of him," he whispered. He stopped and Anne bumped against him. Shutting off the pen light, he took her arm, pointing ahead to where light shone over the top of a dune. They crept forward, covering the last yards on their bellies; Hiller lifted his head and studied the scene below.

There were three air tents spaced around equipment which gleamed under a glare strip. Stanek and two other men squatted close together near the equipment, talking softly. Stanek's companions were weight-room types, their muscles bulging under dusty jump suits. One had very black hair and the other was wearing a skullcap. The three men stood and Stanek and the black-haired one retired to the air tents, leaving the man in the skullcap to settle down at the base of the glare strip. Hiller was about to crawl back when one of the pieces of equipment caught his eye. He took a long look to be sure and then squirmed back, his heart beating faster. At his signal, Anne followed, and when they had put several dunes between them and the camp, Hiller stopped and described what he had seen. "It looks like they've turned in for the night, so we'll do the same. We can look in on them early and see what they're up to."

Anne laid a hand on his arm. "Jared, you're holding something out on me."

Hiller felt annoyance; then grudging respect. "Sorry. It's training and habit, I guess. I've always worked alone."

She nodded. "I'm a reasonable person. From now on, if it makes you feel better the two of us can work alone together."

He smiled, then grew serious. "Remember I said that the equipment looked strange? Well, there was one piece I recognized—a squared-off device about the size of a breadbox. The last time I saw one of them was twenty-five years ago—on the slopes of Mount Goodsir."

Eleven

Hiller awoke late the next morning. Anne was still asleep, her body pressed spoon-fashion against his. The whir of the air unit was a comforting sound, inviting him to roll over and go back to sleep. Instead he looked through the fabric of the air tent and saw that it was day outside—nearly ten o'clock by the sun. He sat up and Anne groaned, rubbing her eyes.

"Whazzit?"

"We've overslept." Hiller felt the adrenalin begin to push the stuffiness out of his head and wondered how he had been able to sleep so long. Anne crawled out of their sleeping bag and began rolling it up.

"I feel dopey," she said. "Could our masks have leaked some monoxides last night?"

Hiller shook his head. "We'd be more than just drowsy; perhaps we were more tired than we thought." He brought out some food sticks and they ate silently. When they had finished, they donned masks, struck the tent, and hid it under some sand. Then they set out for Stanek's camp. Quickly covering the mile they'd left between them, they crawled up the crest of the last dune as they had the night before. When Hiller eased his head over the top he felt a moment's disorientation—the camp was gone. He looked back at Anne and saw their crawl marks in the sand from the night before. Turning again to the depression below, he studied the scoops and ridges in the sand—all that remained to show that someone had visited. If a breeze stirred today, even those marks would be gone by evening.

"What is it?" Anne whispered.

"Stanek got up early today." Hiller took the monitor out of the valise. The light was dead. They stood, brushing the sand off their clothes and staring down at the valley.

"Are you sure this is the place?" she asked.

Hiller didn't answer but picked up his valise and trudged down to the campsite, Anne at his heels. There was not a trace of the men other than the marks in the sand—no bit of waste, strand of rope, drop of machine oil; nothing. Hiller walked back and forth.

"What could they have been after?" Anne asked, watching him pace. "There's nothing here but sand and bugs."

"What was Stanek after on Mount Goodsir?" Hiller countered. "Whatever it was, it was the same thing as here. The two places have to be related, and in some way that would interest the Proteps."

"I've been thinking about that since last night," Anne said slowly.

Hiller nodded. "It might mean that the Proteps have been here longer than five years, when we first met one of their ships off Persephone. At least twenty years longer."

"But we would have seen them—detected any earlier ships. . . ."

"Not necessarily. The Proteps are a big unknown—not just funny-looking blue people with big heads. We don't know what they're capable of."

"What will we do now?"

"We'll settle down on this sand patch until we figure out what it has in common with a mountain in Canada," Hiller said, slapping at a mosquito.

Anne sat down cross-legged. "It sure as hell isn't obvious."

Hiller stared at her. "Nothing obvious. What does that leave?"

"Something hidden—something you can't see."

"Precisely." Hiller got down on his hands and knees and crawled around, peering at the sand.

"Jad . . ."

"It explains the equipment too. Ah, this must be it!" He stopped near where the three men had squatted the night before and began digging in the sand.

"You mean underground?" Anne got up. "That's crazy. You can't dig in this sand."

A shallow conical depression widened slowly under Hiller's hands. "We can't but maybe they can." Anne shook her head and got down beside him. Half an hour passed and their sweat made splotches in the sand before evaporating in the heat. Mosquitoes sensed their increased carbon dioxide output and swarmed around them.

"It's no use," Anne groaned, sitting back on her heels and blotting her forehead. "There's nothing here." Hiller kept digging. Suddenly his hand hit something hard. He scraped the sand back from a small spot of metal. He pounded it with his fist, producing a hollow sound, then sat back and looked at Anne. "This is it."

"Jad, be careful. We don't know what it is. It could be a mine or something."

Hiller shook his head. "It's an entrance." He cleared away more sand until he found a rounded edge. Prying beneath it with his fingers, he tugged until the disc tilted upward, spilling sand into the hole beneath. "It's deep," he reported. "The sides seem to be fused sand—almost like glass, and there are rungs for climbing. I'm going down."

Anne took his arm. "My turn."

He shook his head. "You don't know how to work the photapers and other things," he said as he strapped the valise to his back and edged feet first into the hole.

"What if Stanek comes back?"

"Why should he? Besides, that's your end of it—yell down if you hear a hopter or see anything." She frowned and settled back.

Hiller started down; felt the sudden coolness and adjusted his eye to the dark. Descending at a steady pace, he looked only at the rungs in front of his face. The shaft was a marvel of construction—a perfectly smooth cylinder dropping straight into the earth as though it had been bored with a giant beam of light. Hiller wondered as he climbed what had happened to the immense amount of sand which should have been excavated from such a hole. After a while the motions of his arms and legs became so monotonous that he stiffened in surprise when his foot suddenly hit bottom. As he stepped away from the rungs, light flowed into the shaft from an open archway at his back. He turned and entered a perfectly spherical room. A breeze stirred the hair on his wrist and he lifted his mask, drawing in a shallow breath. The air smelled pure and lightly scented with citrus. Hiller let the mask drop and stooped to examine a hatch in the floor, drawing back when it cycled open. He hesitated, then shrugged and dropped through, landing on a surface which absorbed his fall and then grew hard again. He crouched and peered around, finding himself in an immense round chamber. Buttresses quartered the perimeter and soared upward to join at the center of the vaulted ceiling a hundred feet above the entrance lock. Even though Hiller could find no light source, the walls gleamed like beaten silver and were etched in strange designs—possibly characters or symbols of a language. At regular intervals, arched doorways led into darkened side passages. Beneath a carpet of dust at his feet, pieces of a mosaic pattern glimmered blue and red, but the design was too vast to be assimilated, unless, perhaps, one could have viewed it from the ceiling. Two sets of footprints led away from Hiller, making a jumble of trails further out. He checked to be sure that two sets also led back, then walked across to where the floor dropped away in front of a square of white, set into the wall. The drop-off consisted of tiers descending like rows in an amphitheater. Each tier supported a row of chairs made of the white substance resembling porcelain which he'd first seen in Stanek's apartment. Hiller removed the valise from his belt and sat down in the back row. As if on signal, the opaque surface dissolved; took on depth. His fingers brushed something on the arm of the chair and the screen leaped into focus with a three-dimensional panorama of a city street. A river of human figures flowed between high buildings. The faces in the crowd were mouthing a shout and some were waving signs printed in odd script. The people were unmistakably human and yet their clothes were different from any Hiller had ever seen—skin-tight suits of various bright colors, some iridescent, others alternating in different hues. Hiller pulled a photaper out of his valise and began recording the scene. The sky above the domeless city was hazy and in one corner of the screen Hiller could make out yellow clouds pouring into the air. As he watched, wingless aircraft swarmed suddenly above the throngs and discharged streams of red vapor into the street. The people screamed silently and clutched at their throats, clawing each other in their frenzy to escape.

The scene faded suddenly and was replaced by a solemn-looking old man dressed in a skullcap and a tight-fitting black suit. He sat behind a desk, hands folded, and talked but again there was no sound. Hiller probed at the arm of the chair; colors flashed across the screen and it went dead. After a few minutes he gave up trying to get the picture back and stood, pocketing the photaper.

He looked around the vault. Between the side doorways there were a number of three-dimensional representations set into the wall. He walked over and studied them; most were of machines he could not identify. One was of a globe resembling Earth in its coloration and other features; but with slightly different continental masses and fewer mountain ranges. After taping the globe, he moved to one of the side passages. As soon as he stepped through the nearest arch, a section of hallway lit up in front of him. Doorways were set at ten-foot intervals on both sides as far as he could see. He looked into a few of the rooms; found them all identical—small plain cubicles equipped with a chair, a bed, and a table. As he walked down the silent corridor, sections lit up ahead and winked out behind him. The silence began to be oppressive; Hiller was about to turn back when he encountered a large double doorway marked with two red symbols shaped like drops of blood. The doors slid open in front of him and dust swirled upward from his feet to eddy in the sudden glow from the ceiling. A jumble of rolling cots, machines mounted on wheels, and other scattered equipment lined the walls of a narrow hall which opened onto what looked like sick bays. Hiller entered one of the wards and glanced over the rows of beds crowded together. One of them at the back was covered by a clear rounded shield run through at various points by tubes and wires. With a shock Hiller realized that someone was lying under the shield. Hurrying over he stared down at the mummified remains of a woman. She had died young. White-blond hair spilled around the dried skin of the face and her eyelids sagged inward over empty sockets. Hiller photaped the corpse, then fumbled a C-14 chronometer out of his valise, lifted the shield, and made several passes over the body. As he read the meter, the hairs on his neck rose. He stared at the reading for a long time before a burst of noise shook him. Whirling, he spotted the speaker at once in a corner of the ceiling. A red light was flashing above it and a siren began to wail, followed by a burst of rapid and unintelligible speech punctuated with static.

Hiller moved at once, sprinting out of the room and back through the long corridors. Emerging breathless into the central vault, he saw at once the reason for the alarm. At several places throughout the chamber, small claylike masses had risen like yeast dough from the floor and were pulsating. Though he had never seen anything like them, Hiller noted that they were placed with the strategic precision of an explosives master: suddenly he knew why Stanek and his men had been in the vault.

He raced for the entry sphere, lifted himself through the still-open hatch, and scrambled through the arch into the shaft. Stuffing the photaper into a pocket of his V-coat, he abandoned the rest of the valise. He grabbed the first rungs and started up, arms and legs churning. With nightmare slowness the rungs fell away beneath him; the speck above grew to pea-size, then to the size of a half credit. Each breath burned in his lungs and Hiller realized that his mask still dangled around his neck, but there was no time to stop and pull it up. A rumble began below him and spread up the shaft. With whiplike reports the smooth walls began to crack; a rung broke free above him and glanced off his shoulder as it plummeted past. The hole was ten yards up; now five. Sweat streamed into Hiller's eyes and his warning shout to Anne was swallowed up in a roar. Three yards; two; and then the sound and light died together in a torrent of sand. There was a terrible pressure against Hiller's ribs and then nothing.

Twelve

If it had not been for the artificial arm, Hiller might never have awakened to find his mouth full of sand and one nostril pulling a thin stream of air from somewhere. As it was, the nerve-xylon interface ensured a continuous flow of impulses to the reticular activating system whenever trauma conditions impinged on the sensors of the arm. Almost regretfully Hiller's brain responded and began processing stimuli. He drew in as much oxygen as he could in shallow breaths until his head cleared and pain knifed at his ribs. He checked the position of his right leg; found that it was raised and bent sharply. Gathering his strength, he thrust upward, but sand immediately poured into his free nostril. Panic flooded him; the sand shifted and gave way as he clawed and squirmed to the surface, breaking through with a last convulsive thrust.

For a long time he lay on his back, his chest heaving, before calm returned. Then he raised his head and looked around him; the dunes were deserted—there was no sign of Anne. Easing to a sitting position, he tugged at the cloth of his right trouser leg until the material ripped. He pulled the pant leg off, revealing the synthetic flesh, so perfect with its artificial vein tracings and its thatch of red hair. There was even a scattering of freckles and only a white scar encircling the upper thigh to give away the deception. Hiller tore the pant leg into three strips and bound them tightly around his ribs, sweat tracing streaks through the grime on his forehead as he worked. When he had finished, he pulled the photaper from his pocket and inspected it. It appeared undamaged. Pocketing it again, he got up with the care of an old man. The air burned unfiltered into his lungs, and already Hiller could feel needles jabbing his left side. He called Anne's name; listened to silence, broken only by the hum of insects.

He tried to think. Could the explosions have opened the surface under Anne and buried her? Or perhaps she had followed him down the shaft into the chamber and gotten trapped in one of the side passages. Hiller coughed and spat in the sand; swallowing hard at the sudden lump in his throat. He forced himself to consider his own survival. The hopter held water, food, and most importantly spare masks.

He set off retracing their path of that morning; stopped when he noticed long marks in the sand, as though someone had been dragged. Something hard was pressing against his foot. He knelt; picked up Anne's knife. The blade was clean.

For a time fury dulled his pain, as he thought about what must have happened. Stanek had returned or had carried out an ambush after he, Hiller, had left Anne unprotected. Hiller stared at the knife for a while—first the symbol of her toughness and now of her vulnerability. Then the ache in his ribs seeped back through the anger. He got up and stumbled on, putting one foot before the other until he came to where they had buried the air tent. It was gone. Wheezing from exertion in the acrid air he hurried on to the site of the hopter. Only the twin tracks of the runners remained in the sand. He struck off toward the East.

An hour passed and his tongue began to feel like parchment; the ribs throbbed with every step. Flies began to buzz around his face and to settle brazenly. Crouching for a moment in a bed of weeds, he looked around. The ground was now a mixture of sand and black dirt. Stunted bushes dotted the land around him and he could just detect the sound of flowing water. Getting up, he plodded toward the noise until he stumbled down the bank of a creek. The water was dark and the bottom was strewn with junk. He splashed his face, letting only a bitter trickle into the corner of his mouth. Forcing himself away, he trudged on for a while until he saw the town.

It was a ghost town, of course, too small and poor for a dome. Its inhabitants had all fled decades ago to the cities, leaving their homes and businesses to blacken and decay in the chemical haze. Hiller stumbled forward eagerly. Perhaps someone had left something—a can of food, a jar of water in some old refrigerator—something. Or there might be a mask. Breath rasping, he hurried from building to building, turning over crates, opening cupboards, exploring basements and cellars. There was nothing. He sank down and rested awhile on a broken mattress in one of the houses, staring at a tricycle which reposed upside down on the faded carpet. A thought sank home for the first time with irrevocable force: Earth was finished. He laughed. Was that not the final thought of every dying man—that it was not he but the world which would end? He got up and moved on.

At last the heat brought him to his knees, trembling from loss of water and salt. He coughed and the dirt in front of him was flecked with red. Reaching down, he tried to cover it with loose earth; heard a strange cackling and connected it with the vibrations in his throat. "Just rest awhile," he mumbled, settling onto his back on the baked earth. Slipping off, he dreamed that he was lying in a wasteland instead of safely in his bed; that he was dying of thirst and poisonous air, and that a hopter was beating the sky above him—a shadow blotting out the sun. Waving feebly, he watched it move downward. The dream was quite real now. Hiller could even feel the thump of the landing through the earth at his back, hear the rotors fade below a babble of voices. Then Lieutenant Pierce was looking down at him and shaking his head at Hiller's maskless grin.

"Always got to be a tough guy," he said.

Cool blackness closed in for a while. When Hiller awoke the first thing he saw was a bottle of yellow fluid hanging from a rack above him.

"It's an I.V.," said a voice beside him. "The damn fools were trying to put it in your right arm when I came in."

Hiller turned his head. Pierce was sitting watchfully on the edge of a folding chair. "Hello, Eddie. I don't suppose they have any real food in this place?" Pierce glanced at a medic who hovered nearby. The man came over and read the graphs that were issuing from beneath the bed to pile in neat folds on the floor. He nodded and pulled out the I.V. needle.

"I'll see that you get some food and water, Mr. Hiller. The water will taste a bit salty, but you should drink all of it you can."

Hiller nodded and tried a deep breath. "You've done something to the lung."

The medic paused at the door. "Yes, we did a tracheal fenestration, among other things, while you were unconscious, but the lung's only back to half capacity. There was everything from sulfates to benzpyrene in there. Of course, we only got part of it; we'll just have to wait and see about regeneration." He brightened. "Now the right lung is a different story. Without it, you'd have suffocated for sure. I must say . . ."

Pierce cut him off with an impatient gesture. "Yeah. Our man here is a regular bag of tricks and wonders. Why don't you see about the food?" The medic glared at him and stalked out. Hiller sat up and gingerly probed his ribs. Only a twinge found its way through the cottony layers of paracaine.

"How long was I out?" he asked.

"Thirteen and a half hours," Pierce responded, "and that's the last bit of information you get free. I want to know why you barked knuckles on three of my men just to get yourself out in the middle of nowhere without a mask."

"By the way," Hiller said, "where exactly are we?"

"Unh, unh. I asked you a question."

Hiller smiled and shrugged.

"Maybe you think it's funny. There's a list of unpleasant charges piling up against you. I can make it easy or hard; it all depends. . . ."

"Hold on," Hiller said. "I'm going to tell you enough to get you a captaincy before I'm through." The security man leaned back in his chair, his features settling into an almost comic mask of suspicion.

"Hold the cute stuff. I just want some answers and this time I'm going to get them."

Hiller started to drop down off the bed; Pierce's hand moved and a blaster appeared suddenly in it. "I know you've got moves," he said quietly. "If you take another step toward me, I'll try and hit that tin leg. But I might miss and get you higher up or something."

"Relax. I'm a sick man; besides, I want to tell you. All I ask is that you let me go when I've finished. After all, I haven't really done anything wrong—not that you can prove."

Pierce shook his head patiently. "Hiller, I don't have to prove; you don't even have to have done anything. You know that."

"Still, I want your promise. There's something I have to do, and I'm sure you'll understand when you see what it's all about."

The door opened and an orderly came in with his tray, leaving quickly again in the strained silence. Hiller ate hungrily while Pierce watched. When he had finished, he tossed over the doughnut the PLANESEC agent had been eying.

Pierce grunted. "All right, Hiller. You've got my word," he said between mouthfuls.

"Good. Listen carefully—this is damned important." Hiller told him everything that had happened—why he was following Stanek in the first place, what had taken place at Calgary, and later, at the site of the underground chamber. Pierce watched him intently, interrupting only to clear up certain points. When Hiller had finished, the security man studied him for a minute longer without speaking.

"It sounds like bull," he said at last.

"You can prove it with my photaper." Hiller checked a hand movement toward the front of his hospital gown. "It's in the pocket of my V-coat."

"No it's not."

Hiller felt a stab of dismay. "Then it must have fallen out somewhere. Go back along the route; use as many men as you have to, but find that photaper."

"Don't tell me how to do my job," Pierce said. "What were the co-ordinates where you set down when you were following Stanek?"

Hiller gave him the numbers. "The place they were working

was a few miles due west of there," he added. "The ground was pretty well plowed up, so you should be able to find it."

Pierce motioned at the small mirror above a washbasin in the corner of the room. The door opened and a tall man in a yellow lab coat entered.

"Well?" Pierce said.

"He thinks he's telling the truth."

"Damn it, Pierce. . . ."

"Stay smooth, Hiller. You've got to understand these medical types." The lab man eyed them both clinically and then left. Hiller shook his head.

"Look, I don't know what all this means, but it's gotten too big for me alone. I think it's too big for your outfit, too." He raised his fingers and counted them off. "One: the underground chamber is old; very old. That mummy I scanned dates from the Cenozoic." Pierce frowned and Hiller explained. "That's when the first hominids were supposedly just learning to scratch themselves."

"Hominids?"

Hiller gave up and went on. "Two: Stanek–who works for the Proteps–hunted that chamber down and destroyed it. I've got to believe that's what he was doing twenty-five years ago, when I first met him, and it's a good bet that he's been doing it in various places ever since. That raises more interesting points, like the probability that there are other chambers; like the question of why the Proteps are so intent on destroying them; and the issue of just how long they have been here tampering with the geography before we were formally introduced?"

"It does kind of grab you," Pierce agreed, "even if you throw out any connection with the Proteps, which is just a guess on your part. Let me clear up one other thing. You said that you think your friend Cantrell was kidnaped by Stanek and his crew. Why would they do that?"

Hiller rubbed the knuckles of his right hand. "To find out how much we knew and how much we'd told other people. When they do find out, I wouldn't give a half credit for her chances." His eyes locked with Pierce's. "That's why you've got to let me out of here, now. I'm a trained agent and I know something about Stanek—not much, but more than anyone else. Besides, I've got a personal stake."

Pierce nodded. "Just as soon as I've checked out your story."

"There isn't time. . . ." Hiller sat back as Pierce raised the blaster and moved to the door.

"Just relax. I'll get back to you."

After Pierce left, Hiller examined the room, ignoring for the moment the two-way mirror. There was no way out; the door was three-inch steel and the ventilator duct in the ceiling was too small to crawl into. He turned his attention to the small mirror. Tuning out the reflected light, he looked through into the next room. A guard stood watching; his eyes shifted uncomfortably under Hiller's gaze and after a moment his face disappeared from the window. Hiller moved at once, picking up Pierce's folding chair and bending one of the rear legs back and forth until the hollow steel was ready to snap. Straightening the leg, he replaced the chair and crawled onto the bed, just as the face reappeared at the mirror-window. He ignored the guard after that and sat quietly on the bed, watching the door. Hours passed before it opened again and Pierce entered, blaster drawn.

"We found the site," he said, "but there's no evidence of any explosion. There are a few fragments of fused sand, though. We'll get a crust rig out and see what we can make out with probes."

"What about the photaper?"

"We'll find it if we have to comb every inch you might have gone over."

"Then you believe me?"

Pierce pursed his lips. "Let's just say that for now I don't dare not believe you."

"Good. If you'll get my clothes, I'll be going. You did make a promise. . . ." Pierce didn't move, but looked at Hiller's chest.

"Well, as to that part of it," he said slowly; "I'm afraid I lied."

Thirteen

"Try and understand my position," he went on, still not meeting Hiller's eyes. "We do a security check on a guy named Stanek because he used to do some sensitive work for the government and then he shows up on the Protep payroll. A potentially dicy proposition, you understand, but not out of control. Then you come into it and everything starts to mushroom. Suddenly we've got an intelligent civilization dating to when all the books say our ancestors were tripping over their knuckles. We've got reason to believe that the Proteps have been sneaking around and paying some guys to do funny jobs for at least sixteen years before we invent interstellar drives and run into them outside the solar system—supposedly for the first time." Finally he looked up at Hiller's face. "You're just too hot to let go, man. There are going to be some other people along—big hats. They'll want to ask you things they think I forgot to ask. I'm sure you understand. Don't worry about your friend—I've got plenty of guys out looking for her already. . . ."

"That's not good enough. Those baboons of yours couldn't find their own noses in a yeast mill and you know it."

"I've got some good men, Hiller; they'll find her—if she's still alive."

"You're going to keep your promise, Eddie. Now."

Pierce shook his head and leaned against the door post. "Sorry. Listen, Hiller; you wouldn't like it out there anyway. While you were out collecting gas samples in that plastic lung of yours, things were happening. There's a wholesale riot in Washington, New York's under martial law, same in Chicago, Atlanta, a dozen other citydomes. Stuff's even starting to flare up in Russia."

"Why?"

Pierce shrugged. "You pick it. Some of 'em are at it because Central Authority cut the water ration again. Others are teed off because they can't get better than C-grade soyeast any more on an average income, or because their apartments are being subdivided right across their laps and they're still paying the same rent."

"That kind of thing's been going on for years," Hiller said, wishing Pierce would sit in the chair. "Why is everyone blowing up at once, now?"

"It's the Protep thing. All the xenophobes and Earth's Rights groups have gone berserk since the latest disappearance—that Terran battleship. Looks like they've finally gotten their act together and joined forces. They're picketing every government building all the way up to the executive offices of the World Procurator. Mayor Caviness has closed the exits to Washington or they'd be tearing the Protep embassy to pieces right now. It's the same song—there's a golden gate to paradise out there and the 'sackheads' are keeping us from it. Problems with water, room, food—everything's the Proteps' fault. You know the pitch. . . ."

"I know it," Hiller said. He watched the security man walk to the chair, turn, and stroll back to lean against the door.

"I'll tell you this," Pierce said in a conspiratorial voice; "if it gets much worse, some official knees are going to buckle—especially if it comes down to accepting the blame or letting the aliens have it. There's already enough rubber spines in Geneva for the square-jaws in high command to have an Alliance fleet headed for Eridani inside a week. I hear old bloodyboots Petrov has already put the Seventh on yellow alert." Pierce paused and his eyes met Hiller's. "Can't say I'm against it, either."

Hiller's stomach tightened. He imagined the vast armada building up; thousands of men and women leaving warm beds, meals on the table, their lives, to board the blue and gold shuttles swarming to waiting ships. He could almost smell the ozone and sense the minute vibrations of the ship as the supply silos moved against her sides like great siege engines. But most of all he could feel the molded webfoam of the captain's chair against his back. He realized that Pierce was smiling shrewdly.

"Kind of makes your blood race, doesn't it—Captain?"

Hiller stared at him until the smile slipped. "If they go against Eridani, they won't come back."

"Funny, I had you figured for the adventurous type. Maybe after you get used to being landlocked on Terra for a while instead of cruising around in those big fleet ships, you'll weigh the odds a little different." Hiller thought of the cramped low-ceilinged bridge of the *Trojan* and a corner of his mouth twitched upward briefly. "Of course," Pierce bored on, "if I'd been half blown to Orion like you were, I might be a little battle-shy too. Anyway, we've got a few other odds and ends to talk over before the brass gets here and starts at square one again." He moved back over to the chair, keeping the blaster loosely aimed. Hiller saw that the safety catch was on, with Pierce's thumb resting lightly on it. "I just want to clear up a few points. . . ." Pierce sat; the chair leg Hiller had weakened snapped and the security man pitched backward. Hiller leaped and caught Pierce's gun wrist in his right hand before he could hit the ground. He squeezed; bone grated and the blaster hit the floor. Hiller snatched it, hoisted Pierce with a neck lock as the guard rushed in. He stuck the muzzle under Pierce's ear; the guard hesitated.

"Tell your man to drop the hardware," Hiller advised.

"This isn't going to look good on your record," Pierce wheezed. "I think you busted my wrist."

Hiller glanced down at it. "Just a hairline crack," he said, pushing the muzzle more firmly into Pierce's neck.

"Don't stand there, Kuntz," Pierce croaked. "Drop the damn blaster!" The guard complied.

"Close the door—quietly," Hiller added. "Good; now take off your clothes and just leave the stunner in the side pocket."

Kuntz bristled. "I ain't undressing for nobody," he retorted. Hiller thumbed off the safety and shifted his aim to the guard's groin. "On the other hand . . ." the man said quickly. He stepped out of his jump suit and tossed it on the bed; Hiller released Pierce with a shove and kept the blaster on both men until he had the stunner in his other hand.

"Nap time."

"Aw, for Chrissakes," Pierce protested. "Can't you just leave? I got too much to do. . . ."

"Just hold still," Hiller said, "so I don't get confused and pull the wrong trigger. You can sit down first if you want—it might save a concussion." Pierce glared at Kuntz, who shrugged hopelessly. Both men sat against the wall and the stunner popped twice. Hiller dressed quickly in Kuntz's clothes, drawing the hood around his face and letting the mask dangle at his chin. Pocketing the stunner, he eased the door open a crack and examined the hallway outside. It was deserted. He stepped out, shut the door, and walked down the corridor until he found a lobby, which was empty except for a guard behind a desk who merely looked at him as he passed. When he saw that the lobby door was an airlock, Hiller pulled up the mask and stepped through, pausing outside for a look around. There were two other buildings, squat and solid, and a hopter pad with four craft outlined in the haze. Hiller selected the smallest and walked toward it. A blue-suited figure appeared out of nowhere as he reached the edge of the pad.

"Where do you think you're going, bub?" asked a voice like rock sliding.

Hiller put his hands on his hips and glared. "As you were, sergeant. By God, you're an undisciplined lot."

The big man stepped uncertainly out of the haze and eyed Hiller. "What . . . ?"

"I said AS YOU WERE. You speak when you're spoken to."

"Begging your pardon . . . sir, but I'm to challenge anyone comes into the pad area. Orders from Pierce."

"That's Lieutenant Pierce to you."

"Uh—Lieutenant Pierce. Now, if you'll just tell me who you are, sir?"

"Captain Traver. I'm requisitioning a rig on top-secret business. Stand aside."

The man eyed the bare shoulder of Hiller's stolen uniform. "No, sir. Not without I get some orders first. Lieutenant's laid down standing procedure that I let nobody on the pads without hearing on the phone." He tapped the receiver plugged into one cauliflower ear. "Now, if I could just see some identification," he repeated, drawing his blaster. Hiller reached into the breast pocket of the jump suit, pulled out Kuntz's I.D., and handed it over. When the man's eyes dropped, he chopped at the blaster. Incredibly, the sergeant kept his grip, but the barrel was now sharply bent in the middle. He stared at it while Hiller drew the stunner out of his pocket. "What the hell . . . ?" The stunner popped and he rolled his eyes at Hiller before touching his head to his knees and flopping backward.

Hiller made it to Washington in just over two hours, flying low and following the grid of buried marker signals. He angled the hopter in toward the Protep embassy and set it down half a mile away. Leaving the hopter, he proceeded on foot, moving as fast as his stiff ribs would allow. He topped the last rise before the embassy, halted, and shook his head in disbelief.

The slope was littered with bodies. They sprawled in every direction with the heaviest concentration around the edge of the dome, where they actually lay atop each other. Instinctively, Hiller dropped to his stomach, closing his eyes for a minute and taking several deep breaths to steady his nerves. He looked again. There were hundreds of them, some still clutching lengths of pipe, stones—even furniture legs. A fat middle-aged man lay near him at the top of the slope. Hiller crawled over and groped a cold wrist, finding, to his surprise, a slow but steady pulse. He looked down at the dome. Inside, lines of Proteps filed out of the chancery and other buildings to converge at the exits. Guards in yellow tried to impose order, but knots of confusion sprang up as some of the aliens tried to push ahead. There was a pile of human bodies around the exit, stacked on each other to clear the way to the pads. Every few minutes workers would bring a load of crates and baggage to the lock and return to the chancery, while others would return from the pads and ferry the luggage to three waiting ships, using flat carts which hovered on jets of air. The ground vibrated beneath Hiller and a low rumble issued from the rocket pads. The lines had disappeared, leaving only the workers and a few officials who scurried back and forth across the lawn attending to last-minute details. As Hiller watched, the tall figure of Kotyro strode out the exit lock, golden robes billowing. Some of the glare strips under the dome began to wink out and Hiller realized that there was little time left.

Abandoning caution, he slipped and crawled downward through the bodies until he reached the ones piled by the exit. A party of workers walked by on the other side and Hiller's heart leaped as he recognized Stanek. He made his decision instantly. As soon as Stanek and the others disappeared into the chancery and before the crew from the pads had come back, Hiller jumped up and snapped open a large stand-up case filled with robes and other clothing. Hiding the contents under a pile of bodies, he slipped inside the case and pulled the door shut again. A short time later the crate swayed, lifted, and began to move. The bottom pressed against his feet, signaling an elevator, and then the crate was deposited with a thump. Every few moments the crate slid a few inches as more baggage was piled against it. Then for what seemed a long time there was silence.

When it happened, there was no warning—no vibration through the decks or swell of sound. The slam of acceleration pounded him into the bottom of the case, squeezing the air from his lungs and stripping away consciousness.

BOOK II

Eridani

Fourteen

Hiller did not regain consciousness until the trip was nearly over and the drives had begun their slow planetfall deceleration. He shook his head and blinked in the darkness of the crate. How long had he been out, he wondered? Hours? Days? He shifted, felt a twinge in his ribs through the paracaine deadness. Hours, then; the anesthetic had worn off only a little. But why were they decelerating? Even with the maximum number of hyper-space jumps, Epsilon Eridani III was a journey of days and not hours—but that was for an Earth vessel, he reminded himself.

The G-forces reached maximum, a pressure much below that of the abrupt lift-off, and a jolt passed through the ship as it touched down. Ten minutes later they unloaded Hiller's crate.

He timed a few cycles of noise and silence outside the crate, then slipped out into sunlight. His left eye screwed shut against the glare, he hurried across grass into the shadows of a pavilion which loomed nearby, expecting a shout from behind at every step. None came; he pressed against the cool stone of a column and looked out the way he had come. A party of workers was drawing up on one of the floating carts, with more cargo to add to the pile he'd just left. Beyond them a line of passengers was being processed through an arch which glittered with tubes and wires. A pair of green-suited Proteps supervised the procedure—possibly a medical check, Hiller decided. Flanked by two empty pads, the ship stood about a hundred feet away, its prow incongruously glistening with melting frost. If the two other ships from the embassy had kept pace, they must be orbiting at this moment waiting for debarkation of the first vessel to be completed—a curious waste of fuel and time, Hiller noted. The really surprising thing, however, was the size of the port—only three pads, just as at the embassy on Earth. Assuming that the ambassadorial entourage would land outside a major city rather than some planetary backwater, it was a very small port—a few acres of white surrounded by rolling blue grass and, in the distance, yellow and orange trees. Perhaps there were other pads behind him; Hiller turned and looked through the pavilion to where more of the port was framed between the columns. He could see several buildings—polyhedrons built up from thousands of hexagonal facets to a height of perhaps ten stories. The facets gleamed in the sunlight, changing colors as he watched, and Hiller wondered why the Proteps had been content with such a somber and conventional chancery back on Earth. Was it because they feared exposing even such innocent clues about their culture to the humans?

A few aliens emerged from the nearest building and strolled down the grassy incline toward the pavilion; Hiller edged around the pillar for a glimpse of the remaining area he had not seen. There, in a break between the trees ringing the port, he saw the other ships and nodded to himself. This made more sense; there were dozens of vessels packed close together, shimmering in the heat. Their shapes varied, only a few showing the lean profile Hiller had grown familiar with, and they were really much too close to each other for launching. Intrigued, he measured the distance to the ships and darted glances at the work crew and the Proteps who were approaching from the buildings. Perhaps, if he moved now . . .

He stepped out into the sunshine and almost collided with a short Protep in billowing silver robes, whose approach to the pavilion had been blocked by the pillar. Stepping back, Hiller stalled the upward movement of his arm as the alien merely muttered something and pushed past him. For a moment, reaction locked Hiller in his tracks; he took a deep breath and set out across the grass. Why hadn't the Protep immediately sounded an alarm? Was it possible that he was blind—walking by means of a sensor network? Hiller reviewed the brief image of the alien's face. No, the eyes had peered from under their shelf of bone directly into his for that one instant.

As he covered the last few yards to the pads, Hiller noticed two posts guarding the hedgebreak opening. They looked like the force screen nodes at the embassy gate except that they were dull and pitted. He slowed and reached out a hand before passing unimpeded between the posts onto the hard apron of the pads. The area seemed deserted; he could hear a whisper of breeze through the ranks of the ships; nothing more. The sun baked down and a lemon scent from the trees at the far end of the pad laced the air. Hiller looked around. The ships were indeed packed close together, many resting on the spaces between the raised pads and a few even leaning against each other. Winding his way among the fleet, he craned his neck at the ships. Some showed a sprinkle of meteorite pits along their hulls, but most were smooth—dewboats, as the yardmen back on Earth called unlaunched vessels. Picking out a wide squat ship with some hull marks, Hiller tried the entry lock in its underbelly; it spun open easily and he pulled himself up and through, blinking as deck lights came on.

Swaths of cobweb stuck to his face and draped an untidy sprawl of equipment around the deck. He ran a finger along the back of a molded seat and studied the cake of dust it brought up. The ships were old: despite their shiny exteriors they had sat undisturbed for a long time. Hiller wished for his instruments, buried in the underground vault. Checking some of the equipment, he found an assortment of bulky spacesuits apparently designed to protect against various possible hostile environments. Some possessed gold impregnated visors to screen solar radiation; others had webbed footgear for aquatic worlds and still others were equipped with servomotors useful on high-G planets. Hiller poked around a moment longer, then lowered himself to the pad and looked through several more ships. The results were the same; he settled to his heels on the deck of a very old—and never launched—ship and considered his impressions: the vessels were clearly survey ships, ideal for planetary exploration, high on gadgets and fuel space and low on luxury. But why were they sitting idle on a forgotten slab? Were there no other habitable planets within range of the Protep drives? Hiller rejected the last thought; it was too improbable. The universe was too vast to contain only two Earth-type planets—and those two within a mere eleven light-years of each other. Still, it would make sense of the Proteps' attempts to keep Earth out of space, if, indeed, the Proteps were the ones responsible for the disappearance of seven navy ships. If Epsilon Eridani III was the only other habitable planet within reach of the Earth fleet, then the Proteps had good reason to fear a diaspora of humanity into space. It didn't add up, he decided. There had to be other planets. . . .

Hiller was jarred from his musings by a high-pitched wail which reached him through the open decklock. Dropping through the hatch, he hurried back to the gap in the hedges, shaded his eyes, and peered across the lawn to where a number of Proteps in yellow uniforms had swarmed to the pile of cargo. He thought he could see the gold-robed figure of Kotyro striding up to the group, and as he watched, knots of guards broke away and set off in different directions across the grass. Hiller turned and ran between the ships to the far edge of the field, stopping at the fringe of the trees as his eye caught a familiar shape set apart from the other ships. He stared at the squat vessel for a full minute while the siren wailed and the shouts of the searchers drew nearer. The ship had been made by no Protep hands; its profile was as unmistakable as that of its sister ship, the *Trojan.*

Fifteen

Hiller stared at the gaping hole, surrounded by heat blisters, which made an ugly wound in the flank of the A.S.N. *Hound*. The hole was located on the portion of the ship which housed the Opperman drives. He took a step toward the ship; then whirled and dived into the dense vegetation as footsteps clattered on the far side of the pads.

He ran for a while between limbless dark-blue trunks, which rose like columns, only a few feet apart, and disappeared into a dense thatch of copper-colored foliage above. Finally he halted in a small clearing, waited until his breathing slowed, and listened. The forest was full of sounds—chirping and calling above and a muted babble like flowing water somewhere to his left—but there were no noises of pursuit. He looked up; shafts of white sunlight filtered through gaps in the overhanging leaves and dappled the grass. In every direction around him the smooth boles of the trees crowded together, providing a rich texture of shading and depth. A small golden-haired animal dropped from the canopy of leaves and sat monkeylike on its haunches, regarding him solemnly with luminous brown eyes. Hiller stared back. The animal had no mouth that he could see; its forelegs were short and the paws well developed—almost like hands.

"You wouldn't happen to have a map of this place, would you?" Hiller asked.

"You wouldn't happen to have a map of this place, would

you?" the animal retorted, revealing a thin-lipped mouth that had been hidden under the dense facial hair.

"Well I'm damned," Hiller said, grinning.

"Well I'm damned."

Hiller took a step toward it, holding out his hand, but the creature chittered in alarm and leaped off between the tree trunks. Hiller gazed at his hand and laughed. Then he straightened and wound his way toward the water sounds, coming after a short walk to the banks of a stream. He scooped up a handful of the clear liquid, sniffed it; tasted it. Then he dropped to his hands and knees and gulped the water. He stopped after a moment and wiped his mouth with his sleeve. Something splashed downstream and Hiller glimpsed scales sparkling in a stray shaft of light.

Settling on the bank, he zipped down the front of his jump suit and examined the tape around his ribs. The paracaine was finally beginning to wear off and he took advantage of the remaining anesthetic to adjust and tighten the bandage. Then he leaned back in the grass, letting the hum and buzz of forest life soothe him. He plucked a stem of the blue grass and studied it before slipping it into his mouth. The stem was a lighter blue before it forked an inch from the top into three tips, making a dark blue tuft. The carpet in Stanek's apartment had been an excellent imitation which now fell into perspective.

Hiller sucked the stem, listened to the brook, and gazed up at the coppery leaves, which began about forty feet above his head. The planet seemed to be a paradise, judged from the small sample he had seen. The thought jogged a memory of what Pierce had said only hours earlier: *There's a golden gate to paradise out there and the sackheads are keeping us from it.* The image of the battered *Hound* burned again in his mind. Perhaps the mob was right for once. . . .

For a second another sound mingled with the chortling of the brook. Hiller listened, stilling his breath, until the noise came again—a faint tinkling. He got up and moved toward the sound, surprised at how quickly it swelled. The packed tree trunks must act as a baffle, he decided. He would have to be more wary that the Proteps did not come upon him before he could hear them. The trees thinned and Hiller emerged into a scattered clump of yellow bushes. He looked up, surprised that the sky had dimmed to green-tinged twilight.

Ahead of him the tinkling sound was now quite distinct. It was an intricate melody in flowing bell-like tones; but he still could not make out the source. Then the music cut off and was replaced by an appreciative murmur of voices. Hiller crept up a grassy incline lined at the top by a wall of cone-shaped shrubs. The voices grew louder as he wormed his way into the bushes on hands and knees. The leaves were waxy and smelled of citrus; he pushed through them until they parted over his face.

Bright lights dazzled his eyes and he drew back quickly until he could peer out through the foliage unseen. Spread on a trimmed slope below were five low silver tables surrounded by reclining Proteps robed in bright colors. Above them at a height of about thirty yards, three brilliant discs floated against the afterglow of sunset. There was a building—apparently a dwelling—at the crest of the slope; more of the waxy shrubs, lit at the base by ground lights, hugged the house's cream-colored walls. A platform stood outside the door; the musician had just turned from an instrument like a sculpted sunburst and was conversing with a lean white-robed Protep who stood in the doorway.

The musical sounds of the alien language rolled in the scented air; fountains at the corners of the house chortled and blew spray under the lights. Occasionally a guest would raise a small golden tube and mist would glitter before dissipating on the breeze. Delighted cries and peals of hoarse laughter began to rise from the tables; at intervals, a blue head would bob appreciatively or a hand would lift as though to embellish some story. Hiller sniffed and the now familiar scent of intoxicant mingled with the tart odor of the bushes. As he watched, the figure in the doorway clapped his hands once and stepped aside, making room for a procession bearing trays piled high with food. Hiller stared at the servers, his pulse quickening. They were humans.

Then a voice spoke behind him and someone kicked him in the heel.

Sixteen

Hiller thrashed upward through the tangle of shrubbery and backed out awkwardly to the accompaniment of laughter. It took him a second to realize that it was not the harsh grating laughter of a Protep. He turned and confronted a young woman who looked about twenty. Her hair fell in soft black ringlets onto the sheer material of her robe and there was an amused expression on her lips.

"*Sor turi Kzorintus?*" she asked.

Hiller shook his head and shrugged at the same time, making her laugh again. He started past her but she laid cool fingers on his arm.

"Look, lady," he said, "I'd like to stay and chat, but your masters are sniffing along my trail and I'd prefer not to be caught just yet."

"Ah," she said. "The American stowaway—Hiller. I thought so." Her English was flawless. She inspected the dusty blue uniform and then studied his face. "Handsome," she added in a speculative voice. Hiller flushed.

"You're from the United States?" he asked.

"You might say I did my time there before retiring. My name is Ilise." She held out her hand and Hiller took it uncertainly.

"That's an odd way of putting it. Retired from what?"

"Oh, I was secretary to the World Procurator."

Hiller thought about that. "And in return for certain information supplied at regular intervals, the Proteps offered you the rest of your life in paradise."

She laughed, still holding his hand. "You sound so disapproving, Mr. Hiller."

"Oh no. I heartily approve. What's a sellout compared to all this?" He withdrew his hand and waved it around. "Lawn parties, nice clothes, grass under your feet, and pure sky over your head. So what if you have to wait tables once in a while. Tell me, Ilise, are they nice to you? What about the folks back home on Earth? Do you ever miss them? But no; I guess you wouldn't —not with all this."

"Why, Mr. Hiller. I believe you're trying to irritate me." She moved closer to him and he caught a whiff of perfume as she put a hand on his hip and slid it around to his back.

"Or maybe there wasn't anybody to leave behind. It would make better sense. That way there's no homesickness. Is that how it was with you and the others?"

"We left no one behind," she admitted coolly.

Hiller felt a stab of irritation. "What else did they do for you? Surely they didn't just walk up and say 'how would you like to do a little espionage work for us?' Let me guess: they recruited you in a hospital." He looked into her startling green eyes, now only inches away. "They gave Martin Stanek a new arm. What did they give you, a new face?" He realized the illogic of it as soon as he said it: Stanek had been working for the aliens before they restored his arm. He felt a perverse pleasure anyway.

Ilise stepped back and frowned. "Really, Mr. Hiller, you are being very unpleasant. . . ."

"That raises another subject," he said. "How do you know my name? As far as your masters know, I'm buried about three hundred yards deep in an unmarked grave. They know someone stowed away, but how do they know it was me . . . unless . . ." He trailed off. What if one of Pierce's men was a Protep agent? Ilise was still pouting.

"Oh, it's been all over the ComWeb," she said irritably. "How should I know what made them believe it was you? Why don't we forget all this unpleasantness and start over. I'll bet we could become good friends."

Hiller looked around, feeling exposed, but they were still alone; the voices from the party still drifted peacefully through the shrubbery. "Won't someone be missing you down there?"

"It's not my turn," she whispered, closing in. Hiller was thinking of ways to extricate himself when a small golden rod appeared suddenly in her hand, apparently from a hiding place in her sleeve. Before he could react, she had laid it against his temple. He felt his breath quicken and his heart begin to pound as the animal smell of her filled his nostrils. Her hand caressed the nape of his neck; drew his head forward. Her lips were warm and sweet; he could feel the swell of her breasts even through the tape and returning soreness of his ribs. The golden rod fell unnoticed into the grass.

Afterward she rolled away from him and lay naked on the lawn while he pulled on his jump suit with slow befuddled movements. He zipped up the front of the suit and sat unmoving, while the cries and clatter of the party grew more raucous in the background. After a while Ilise sighed and shivered in delight; got up in a sinuous movement and shrugged back into her gown as Hiller watched.

"That was good," she said, cupping Hiller's chin in her hand.

"What did you do to me?"

She laughed merrily. "You enjoyed it, didn't you?"

Hiller's head began to clear. He remembered the golden rod and looked around until his eye caught a gleam in the grass. She scrambled for it at the same time, but Hiller got there first, clutching the rod.

"Give it back," she demanded.

Hiller crushed it.

"Now you've done it, you . . . you . . ."

"Bastard?" Hiller suggested.

"That will do until I think of something worse."

"I don't like being a puppet," Hiller said. "Most women have been content to rely on their charms; do you doubt yours so much?"

She scowled at him. "You do say such horrid things. I've got half a mind to scream right now. That enhancer was given to me by my Provider, Tuoro, on my twenty-fourth birthday."

"I'm sure he'll give you another, if you're a good little girl."

A tear trembled at the corner of her eye. "Tuoro is dead. It was hor—horrible. He . . ." She shook her head and buried her face in her hands. Hiller watched her, feeling oddly touched.

"We all die," he said softly.

"You don't understand at all, Mr. Hiller," she said coldly, dropping her hands. "Tuoro was so good and kind—so wise. Then he killed himself. In an acid bath. They couldn't even . . ."

"Did you love him very much?"

She nodded. Hiller tried to understand, to envision an old Protep with wrinkled blue skin who would take an Earth girl under his wing, but the effort broke down when it came to him presenting her with the enhancer.

"I'm sorry I ruined your toy," he said, "but you really should learn to do without it. A woman as lovely as you . . ."

She brightened. "Why, thank you. I do believe that's the first nice thing you've said. Shall we celebrate with some food and wine?" Hiller suddenly felt ravenous. How long had it been since he'd eaten? A meal at the PLANESEC base almost a day ago was the last time. His knees felt suddenly weak and the juices began to flow in his mouth. She took his hand. "Come along then."

"Where are we going?"

"Don't worry. We won't be seen."

She led him around behind the wall of shrubbery to a row of low buildings which glowed softly in the darkness. Ilise stepped into the wall, Hiller hanging back on her hand, and a space opened in front of her. They walked through.

Hiller looked warily around. "Is this real or did I just walk through some kind of projection?"

"Oh, it's solid enough." She smiled and sat down on a curving divan placed along one wall of the spacious room, patting the space beside her; but Hiller was still investigating. The ceiling was high and curved rather than cornered. Under his feet, the tile floor was softer than any carpet. There were few articles of furniture—only the standard divans, a chair, and a heavy looking crystal table.

"What's your pleasure?"

Hiller thought a moment. "Well, a nice yeast steak, high grade of course, would be good for starters. . . ."

"Come now, Mr. Hiller. Surely you can be more imaginative. This isn't Earth, you know. Would you like Chateaubriand with a nice Bordeaux or perhaps an all-American porterhouse about one and a half inches thick would be better. . . ."

Hiller's mouth twisted. "No thanks. I don't think I'm up to it after all these years."

"Oh, it's all made in the cloning tanks, of course. No animal is ever slaughtered. The cuts are grown by RNA analogue templates. . . ."

"Just the same, I'd better stick to basics," he said. She shrugged, nodded at the crystal table, and Hiller looked around just as a steaming plate of yeast steak popped into view. Aware that she was watching in amusement, Hiller went over to the table and matter-of-factly began to eat. The food was excellent and he could not remember when he had enjoyed eating more. He chewed slowly and sipped the red wine Ilise had conjured to go with the yeast steak. When he had finished, the dishes disappeared.

"Why don't the masters use these gismos for the lawn party," he asked, "instead of making your friends into servants?"

"That's the third time you've called them masters," she said. "It's not like that at all. You keep thinking in Earth terms and that won't get you far here. It's an honor to serve them on these ceremonial occasions—but you wouldn't understand that."

"No, I guess not." He sat down at the other end of her divan. "Earth is polluted, depleted, overcrowded, and deprived, but at least there are no slaves there."

"That's a pretty sentiment," she replied. "You evidently haven't lived on the lower levels or tried to subsist on a grade-seven income. There are millions of people down there who would sell their souls into slavery for more living space or an extra daily ration of soyeast. Some of them do, too; but at least they're not called slaves."

He looked at her and tried to form a reply. What could she know of Earth—a pampered Procurator's secretary who had used her position to betray her race. "At least you made a better deal than the rest when you sold out," he said finally.

"Come, Hiller. We decided not to quarrel." She slid over to him and ran her fingers along his chest. "I'll bet those are sore," she said, probing the ribs gently.

"I've had worse," he said shortly.

"Come on over here," she said with a tolerant smile. She rose gracefully and tugged at his hand. He followed her to a wall; she touched it in two places and a panel slid aside revealing a mass of gleaming clear tubes feeding into an opaque flattened cone the size of a dinner plate. The cone drifted out of the wall and hovered over his chest like a strange animal, sniffing. Lights twinkled and a few of the tubes writhed briefly; then the apparatus withdrew into its niche. Hiller felt his ribs in amazement. They were completely healed.

"Now let's take this nasty old bandage off," Ilise said, zipping down his jump suit and unwinding the tape. Hiller drew in a deep breath. Even the tickle in his left lung was gone. He shook his head and then grabbed Ilise's wrists where they had descended toward his groin.

"That's enough."

"But you said I should use my own charm," she pouted. He zipped up the jump suit.

"Use it on one of your friends when they're done playing at busboy."

"Those *castrates?*" She studied him for a moment, a finger pulling down her lower lip to reveal even white teeth. "I know what it is," she said at last. "You're in love with someone; that woman they captured, perhaps."

Hiller looked up sharply. "What woman?"

"The spy. Anne Cantrell."

Seventeen

"Eeeach! *Fau kierr*—you're hurting me!"

Hiller realized that he held her shoulders in a viselike grip; he let his hands drop and she rubbed at the red marks. "I'm sorry," he said. "What do you know about Anne Cantrell?"

"Then it's true. You are in love with her."

"I—we are friends. What did you mean, calling her a spy?"

"Why, simply that she is one of those people who snoop around under false pretensions. I used the word correctly. . . ." She frowned, and in his impatience Hiller missed the discordant cue.

"No, no," he snapped. "Spying where? On whom? For what purpose?"

"I shouldn't be talking like this," she said. "In fact, I should be reporting you." A hint of calculation had crept into her voice. She looked him up and down as if inspecting a faulty piece of goods. "After all, you've insulted me, spurned my affection, ruined a precious keepsake, and physically threatened me, despite the fact that I have protected and fed and healed you. I thought it would be nice to help you—after all, you are a human being; and despite what you think, there are certain loyalties."

"I appreciate—"

"But I can see I've been wrong." She traced a finger up the midline of her gown, closing it almost to her neck, and the gesture was not lost on Hiller. He stepped close to her, putting his hands on her waist.

"I'm sorry." Still she held back, but her eyes softened a little. Hiller reached up and pulled the gown open again, releasing the firm round breasts. She drew in her breath and moved against him. Hiller lowered her to the floor.

When he rolled away a few minutes later he felt only a vast exhaustion. The floor molded itself to his back and he had to close his eyes because they refused to focus properly. For a moment, he stared through the red veil of his right lid at the ripple of Ilise's ribs beside him; then he damped out the afferent nerves and slid into a deep trough while part of his mind settled around an image of Anne and waited.

When he awoke, he was still on the floor. A blanket had been drawn over his shoulders; he fingered it sleepily for a moment before looking up to find Ilise curled on the divan studying him.

"When I was on Earth, I always wanted a blanket over me when I slept," she explained. "Maybe it was security or something."

He noticed that she was dressed in a severely modest gray gown. "How long have I slept?"

"Eleven hours."

Hiller groaned and sat up, rubbing his eye. "I've got to get out of here."

"Why? You're safe here. No one ever comes into another person's presence uninvited—it's a social taboo. If you go out, you'll just get caught."

"Do you mean that the Proteps won't search for me in people's homes?"

"Not unless they actually saw you go in while they were pursuing you."

"Then I could be hidden indefinitely."

"Yes. But they would not expect anyone to do that. If someone told them you were here, they might wait outside until you left, but they would never enter uninvited just on the word of someone else."

"You said they wouldn't expect anyone to protect me—does that mean that even most of the humans on Eridani would turn me in?"

"Yes."

"Then why don't you?"

She considered for a moment. "I was going to—as soon as you no longer . . . amused me. But now I can't." She looked away for a moment, then turned back, her face composed. "You have offered me the gift . . . of your friendship. . . ." She trailed off, as if conscious of how lame it sounded. "Just let it be. I won't turn you in."

He looked at her thoughtfully. "Just the same, I can't stay."

"I know. It's the woman—Anne Cantrell. You are more than just friends." Hiller nodded and she looked away again. "I'm going to tell you all I know. No, don't say anything. Here it is: it's been on the ComWeb since the legation returned—how they caught the two of you on embassy grounds. They captured her, but you escaped and stowed away. They say you have a transmitter and will try to send messages back to Earth as you discover important military and . . . sociological information."

"It's not true."

She contemplated him. "I searched your suit while you were asleep—I wasn't going to turn you in, I just had to know. If there's a transmitter, you must have hidden it in the woods."

"What have they done with Anne?"

"Oh, she's all right. They brought her back on one of the ships. They want to try both of you together, so they're holding her in the citadel."

Hiller felt a surge of frustration. Anne might have been on the same ship with him. "This citadel," he said. "Will you show me where it is?"

She got up and walked to a place at the wall; touched open a large space lined with books. Hiller stared. Only in Earth museums had he seen so many of the bulky things together at once. Her finger ran along the spines, stopping at a volume wider than the rest. Pulling it down, she laid it on the floor beside Hiller and thumbed through brightly illustrated pages of maps until she found the one she wanted. She touched a corner of the page and the map leaped into three dimensional focus. Hiller shook his head and fingered the thin page; the illusion of depth and topography was perfect.

"We are here," she said, pointing. "The citadel is here—about six of your miles away. Between is this brashery stand." Hiller examined the miniature stretch of foliage.

"I know. The smooth trees packed all together."

She smiled. "Not trees; tree—it's all one tree with a central trunk underground. Those things you thought were trunks are just branches sticking up above ground."

"And I suppose those little gold creatures who like to mimic are the true rulers of Eridani," Hiller said.

"The Opachii?" This time she laughed. "They're about as bright as a jack rabbit, but a good deal more gifted vocally. I'm surprised you saw one—they're very shy."

"Is there anything else in the forest—in the tree, that is—that I should know about? Something not so shy and harmless?"

"No. You said it yourself. Eridani is a paradise."

Hiller studied the area around the citadel a moment longer. "Can you tell me any more about where they're keeping Anne?"

"Only that there are lots of ceremonial doors—you shouldn't have to cope with walking through walls." He closed the book and she caught his hand. "You can't do it. The place will be thick with guards—Proteps, not softhearted humans like me. They may be expecting you; why else would they broadcast where they're keeping her?"

"That thought crossed my mind."

"She may not even be there."

Hiller nodded. "Have you got any clothes that might make me less conspicuous?"

She hesitated and then smiled. "As a matter of fact, yes. The last time Rik . . . was here, he left his cowl." She opened a wall closet and shook out the garment as Hiller finished zipping up the jump suit. He put on the robe and drew the hood over his head, nodding in approval. She handed him a small bag of brown squares and steered him to a place in the wall, not meeting his eyes. "The stuff in the bag is food. Go through here." He reached out but she had turned away. He swallowed his parting words and stepped through the wall into a deserted courtyard.

He tried to shake off a touch of foreboding as he crossed the yard, his hand clutching the cowl together at his throat. Ilise was a source of data, the meaning of which he had not yet uncovered. Thinking back over the past few hours, he tried to pry loose some buried insight that would make sense of her. Why had she not betrayed him? Friendship, she had said. Was it a euphemism for sex, and if so, why did she value the act so highly? She was attractive; wasn't he wearing at this moment a cloak left by one of her lovers? The questions circled fruitlessly as he made his way to the wall of shrubs which ringed the estate. The remains of last night's feast were still spread on the silver tables. A napkin flapped idly in the breeze; Hiller squinted at the sun, still low on the horizon, and then worked his way through the coppery bushes, leaving the house behind. Evidently the humans were not quite as servile as they had seemed the night before, or surely they would have had the grounds cleaned up by now. Hiller remembered Ilise's remarks about a ceremonial occasion. There was much he could have learned from her had he stayed; how the other humans had been recruited, what their functions had been on Earth; not to mention vital data on the Protep civilization. What was it she'd said? Military and sociological information. *Odd, that last.*

He crossed the undulating ground between the hedge and the brashery stand and plunged into the forest, as he still insisted on regarding it. The rays of the sun slanted twenty yards into the edge of the thicket, cutting the grass into strips of light and shadow before dissipating among the packed trunks. He trudged along in silence for a while, nibbling one of the food squares—which was surprisingly good—and depending on feedback loops in his right leg to keep him walking in an approximate straight line toward the citadel. The light deeper in the thicket was quite dim; however, a host of green birdlike creatures in the leaves above him had caught the morning light and begun chirping and thrashing about. Otherwise the forest was silent save for the swish of his feet through the grass. So faintly came the new sound that he stopped without really knowing why and zipped the throat of the jump suit open beneath the cowl. It came again, this time reaching consciousness; a soft thunk-thunk in front of him. Remembering how quickly the dense boles dampened sound, Hiller moved forward cautiously until the trunks parted a few yards in front to reveal a large clearing.

Hiller studied the space from behind a trunk, trying to decide why it seemed wrong to him. It could be a natural phenomenon—an area where for some reason the brashery branches could not thrust aboveground, but he did not think so. A stringent smell, like sap, came suddenly as the breeze changed directions, and Hiller looked more closely at the deep grass near the edge of the clearing; bits of white like the tops of newly cut stumps showed through in several places. Instinctively, he backed a few steps into the woods, noticing the silence for the first time. The foliage above him hung still, undisturbed by the bird-creatures, and nothing but the wind stirred the grass in the clearing. There had been no recurrence of the sound that had drawn him in the first place. Something was wrong here, but he couldn't risk investigating—not with Anne waiting liberation from the citadel prison.

Hiller turned, then dropped into the grass as something hissed above the canopy of leaves. A shadow rippled in the grass of the clearing as a huge brick-shaped craft slowed to a hover and began to descend on jets of air. A port cycled open in the wingless ship as it settled the last few feet, and a section of ground nearby rose like a trap door. The engines died with a final gust and a line of robed and hooded figures began to descend, making their way to the trap door and disappearing into the ground. Hiller peered in surprise at the faces under the hoods—they were black and smooth as stones. Then he realized that all of the figures were wearing masks. He wondered briefly if they were humans, but the hoods were too well filled out; the space above the eye-slits too great. He counted fifty-seven of the figures before the port finally cycled shut. The slab of earth fell back into place as the craft rose straight up and zipped out of sight.

Hiller started to get up, sensing a movement behind him at the last instant before darkness closed in.

Eighteen

"My dear Hiller, you mustn't be too hard on yourself." Kotyro sipped green frothy liquid from a tumbler and gazed at Hiller. "It's quite amazing that you were able to avoid capture as long as you did. As a matter of fact, that's one of the things we'll be wanting to discuss in more detail, I'm sure."

Ignoring the throbbing behind his left ear, Hiller looked across at the former ambassador, who reclined at ease on the larger of two divans, a silver enhancer dangling negligently from one hand. The enhancer was a slightly larger model than the one with which Ilise had so easily controlled him. There were no guards in the small windowless room; perhaps if he moved quickly enough . . .

Hiller stiffened and pitched sideways against his divan, arms and legs locked. Kotyro kept the enhancer leveled at him for a moment, then let it drop. Hiller sagged.

Kotyro clucked deep in his throat. "Believe me, Captain, I regret that your civility must be doubted in so undignified a fashion; however, certain rumors and facts about your remarkable capabilities have not escaped our attention." The alien's eyes glittered in their deep pools and he smiled, revealing small bluish teeth. Hiller wondered if such baring of the teeth was more or less ambiguous in Proteps than in humans. "You are considering my use of effect," the alien said. "You think that I maneuver for the psychological advantage." Hiller felt the hairs stir on the back of his neck. First Kotyro had anticipated perfectly his move for escape and now he was reading his mind.

"You are a telepath?"

"Not at all; though if I truly wished to overwhelm you, it would be simple enough to let you think so. No, Captain, the fact is that I have no need of artifice. I know very much more of you than you of me—a fundamental inequality that ensures all outcomes between us will end as I wish."

Hiller let the remark pass. If it was true, then he was doomed in any case. If not, it represented overconfidence—a weakness which he might be able to exploit. "Where is Anne Cantrell?"

"Right here in the citadel. You should see her soon enough—unless I have overestimated you."

Hiller digested the cryptic remark; decided that he didn't like some of its implications.

"Why did you bring me here," he asked, "when you had an installation thirty yards from where I was captured?" Kotyro studied him and Hiller sensed that he had scored a hit.

"That is a strange question, Captain. Why should we not bring you here? Would you take a prisoner of yours on Earth to a Mason's lodge?"

Hiller raised an eyebrow, surprised at the depth of Kotyro's knowledge of human social groups. "You expect me to believe that hole in the ground is some cozy little clubhouse?"

"Has something convinced you that it is not?" Kotyro countered. "Tell me, Captain; what do you think it is?"

"I don't know."

"Perhaps you would care to guess, then."

Hiller felt a touch of *déjà vu*. His mind leaped back thirty-five years to a hot summer day outdome in East Milwaukee. He and his pal Jerry had hooked their fathers' masks and gone exploring through one of the vast municipal dumps outside portal 16. Under a large mound of trash they had found a tunnel leading inward to a large room supported by scrap-metal struts, and furnished with decayed couches, warm beer, comics, and pin-ups. He remembered how Jerry and he had stared at each other in wonder, knowing from a large emblem on one wall that they had found the secret hideout of the Fighting Wildcats gang. They'd hung around for a few minutes feeling important and scared, and were picking their way out of the dump when they saw five boys, dressed despite the heat in leathersim jackets. The boys had fanned out and were coming for them.

"Just act natural," Jerry had quavered, his adolescent voice cracking. Little Jad, two years younger, had nodded and swallowed hard. Then the bigger boys were upon them, forming a tight semicircle and brandishing an assortment of short chains, brass knucks, and switchblades. The leader had chewed his gum like tridee tough guy Rocky Buckner for a moment and then snarled, "What you punks t'ink you're doing back here?"

"Just looking around," Jerry had said, his voice rising to a squeak on the last syllable. Jad had winced inside, knowing it was precisely the wrong answer.

"Izzat so?" the tough had replied. "See anyt'ing interesting?"

"No," little Jared had said then with surprising firmness.

"No." Hiller said now, and wondered if it would work better on the alien than it had on the kid back in Milwaukee. Kotyro looked at him.

"You took rather a long time to answer, Captain. I wonder if you are being entirely candid with me."

"Just daydreaming."

"An excellent strategy, but difficult to maintain under certain circumstances." The glass disappeared as Kotyro set it on one of the ubiquitous crystal tables. The alien studied his enhancer a moment, rolling it between a bony thumb and forefinger. "I'll be frank, Captain. What I may have to do distresses me a great deal, but I intend to get certain information from you at any cost. You will both determine and pay that cost. If you refuse to co-operate you will face more pain than any human has ever endured."

"And if I co-operate?"

"You will live in comfort for the rest of your life."

"In a Protep prison?"

Kotyro shrugged. "I hope that alternative will seem as attractive to you now as it most assuredly will later, if you do not co-operate. I have no wish to inflict needless pain on you. If you are going to tell everything anyway, then why not do so right away?"

"What are your questions?"

"Good, good." Kotyro sat up on the divan and arranged the golden robe around his knees. "You did a good deal of spying while you were on Earth and ultimately were able to follow Martin Stanek to a certain underground chamber. Now, we know of your history in Naval Intelligence and of your proficiency with a number of rather specialized devices which you frequently carry around with you. We would like to know just what you discovered in the chamber and what items you recorded with your photaper."

"Has it been found?" Hiller asked.

"Pierce's men are still looking for it. If it is found, we will know."

"You have lots of people on the payroll, don't you, Kotyro. How do you keep them all honest?"

"What is on the photaper, Captain?"

"I don't remember. The explosion and cave-in wiped out most everything I'd seen down below."

"That is a lie."

"Why do you care what is on the photaper? What is it about those chambers that is so dangerous to you?"

"Not to us; to you. If your race discovers what is in the *Uluspansa,* they will be in very grave danger."

"And because you are so altruistic, you wish to save us? Come now; isn't it the other way around? You are determined to put us in danger if we discover the meaning of the vaults. . . ."

"My patience wears thin. Are you going to answer my questions?" Hiller settled back on his divan and studied the ceiling. "Perhaps we should try something different," Kotyro said after a moment. "Where have you hidden the transmitter?"

Hiller stared at him. "There isn't any transmitter."

"Again, you are lying," Kotyro snapped. "You expect us to believe that you, an experienced espionage operator, slipped unnoticed aboard our vessel with nothing but the clothes on your back? We know that your Navy has developed a narrow beam transmitter for your new Opperman ships. Our intelligence reports indicate that the transmitters are quite small; you could easily have boarded with one. We do not doubt in the slightest that you did precisely that. What messages have you sent? What is the ultimate purpose of your mission?" Kotyro was leaning close now and Hiller could smell the faint meaty odor of his breath. He was surprised at the depth of Kotyro's information—the narrow-beam transmitters were a closely guarded secret. The aliens were wrong on one detail, however; the transmitters were certainly not small enough for one man to carry. Hiller realized that Kotyro was watching him expectantly.

"Go to hell."

Kotyro shook his head almost sadly and got up. "Let it be on your head, Hiller. Remember, you could have dealt with me." He swept out of the room as another Protep entered. The new alien was about five feet tall, soft skinned, and smooth of forehead. His flesh was a darker variant of the usual blue and his mouth a thin slash which curved downward across the lean jaw. He was clothed in tight-fitting black and one small gloved hand held a foot-long metal rod.

"Ah, Hiller," he purred in a soft tenor. "I am delighted that your intransigence has permitted us to meet. My name is Sarko, in case you should later wish to lodge a complaint." His slender neck vibrated beneath the suit's high collar as he snorted at his own joke. He tugged at the cuffs of his gloves and eyed Hiller for a moment. "I am obliged to offer you a final chance, human, and I must say I hope you do not take it." Sarko said "human" as if it were a filthy word and Hiller could sense an almost personal hatred beneath the alien's composure. "There are three questions. You have already heard them in part and there will be others. Before we start, there are certain preliminaries." Sarko paced back and forth in front of Hiller, slapping the metal rod against one palm. "We are aware, Captain, that certain areas of inquiry may arouse preconditioned blocks in your mind. Some of these blocks can be broken by my techniques; others, if pressed too severely, will result in the stoppage of your heart. I shall try to be careful that death does not intrude prematurely on our deliberations; nevertheless, it will be best if you adopt a co-operative frame of mind."

Sarko stepped back and leveled the rod at Hiller. "To demonstrate that this is not like Kotyro's toy, I will now make a simple suggestion: You are on fire."

Hiller leaped backward off the divan and fell writhing to the floor as the flames raced up his pant legs and seared his chest. He beat at them and rolled over and over, but the fire only grew worse, crackling and licking at his face. Someone screamed horribly; his lungs turned into a blast furnace and the plastic skin of his face began to melt. Then Sarko said, "Enough," and the fire was out. Hiller found himself on the floor, his lungs heaving and his V-coat soaked with sweat. Sarko gave him a minute; then told him to get up. Hiller stood slowly, inspecting his clothes as part of his mind clung to the illusions.

Sarko smiled. "As you can see, the effect is quite perfect; for all purposes you actually were on fire, the details supplied by your own mind. The beauty is that you can experience endless pain of every description while your body lives on, preserving your secrets until you beg to tell us. Of course, as I noted earlier, there are certain risks—heart failure, shock."

Hiller sat down on the divan and forced himself to breathe deeply.

"Good," Sarko said. "You will last a long time. Now let us return to my three questions: One, what did you record on the photaper? Two, where did you hide the transmitter and what have you signaled back to Earth? Three, who on this planet aided you in avoiding capture?"

For a moment Hiller did not answer; an important piece of data was pushing at the edge of consciousness—something about the transmitter. He concentrated but it would not come. "That was actually four questions," he said at last. Then he was foundering in the ocean; going down, the water pouring into his lungs and choking him. After a moment the reassuring bulk of the divan pressed once more against him and Sarko was studying him as he drew in a gasping breath.

"That is for your impudence. Now, what is on the photaper?"

It went on like that for a time. Hiller's evasions broke slowly into bits of truth. Twice he was able to black himself out by hyperventilating, but both times Sarko merely waited patiently until he regained consciousness and then punished him. After a while, Hiller told him what was on the photaper—the scenes played out on the viewscreen, the globe that looked much like Earth, the mummified woman that was over twelve million years old. He held out much longer before he told the alien about Ilise; when that happened he wasn't really aware of it. Sarko let him rest for a bit, and he imagined his hands around the alien's bird neck, savored the feel of it snapping under his thumbs.

"You've done quite well, Hiller," the alien said. "But we still have one question before we can rest. Where is the transmitter? You have been very stubborn on this one but you will tell me, just as you have answered the other questions."

Hiller gazed dully at the alien while his mind calculated. A show of weakness could only help him now. Sarko would not believe that there was no transmitter and he dared not go too far until he knew where it was hidden and what messages Hiller had sent. The alien stepped forward and slapped him lightly with a gloved hand.

"Where is the transmitter?"

"There is no transmitter," Hiller said wearily. He felt the Protep's eyes study him.

"Very well; perhaps it is time for another approach." Sarko motioned and two lean aliens entered on cat's feet and gripped Hiller from either side. He let himself droop against them, moving his feet spasmodically as they half-carried him from the room into the corridor outside, Sarko leading the way. Beneath the sham he tested himself, flexing muscles, co-ordinating small movements, and breathing in long slow breaths. After a short walk they turned off the corridor into another small room. Hiller felt the negligent grip of the two guards and readied himself. Sarko turned to face him; Hiller's eyes focused on the blue sandaled feet.

"Well, Hiller, wouldn't you like a look around?" The alien

grabbed a fistful of Hiller's hair and jerked his head up, directing his eyes toward the center of the room. There, in the company of another small Protep dressed like Sarko, was Anne Cantrell.

Nineteen

The soft brown hair was mussed and her face was very white. She was dressed in a tan jump suit of alien make.

"Hi, Jared," she said brightly, but her chin quivered for just a second. Hiller tried to say something but his throat constricted and he simply grinned at her. His eyes flickered around the small room; in addition to the ones who had brought him, there was the other black-suited Protep and that was all. None of them were armed with anything he could identify as a weapon—Sarko appeared to have left the metal rod behind.

Hiller threw both arms outward and the guards stumbled back. Tearing his right arm free, he swept a roundhouse that caught the guard on his left across the skull and sent him flying against the wall. Hiller pivoted on the left leg and caught the second guard with a straightened foot in the stomach before the third alien was halfway to him. Sarko tried to rush by him to the door; Hiller grabbed the black jump suit and it tore down the front, pulling him off balance into the guard's path and knocking both aliens sprawling. The one who had been with Anne tried to get up, caught a kick under the jaw, and settled to the floor, heels rattling. Sarko scuttled backward until he came up against the wall.

"Don't . . . don't," he gasped. The second guard was just now pitching forward, both hands gripping his stomach. He hit face down and the room was deathly still. The whole thing had taken perhaps four seconds.

Anne ran over and threw her arms around Hiller, her body trembling against his. "Nice work, Hiller. I want you to teach me that second kick."

Hiller laughed—an adrenalin cackle which sounded loud in his ears. "I've got to save something," he said, "in case I ever have to fight you." Sarko started to get up. "Stay put," Hiller snapped, and the alien settled back.

"You will regret this, Captain," he said in a low voice. Hiller stared at the withered mammaries on Sarko's chest where the cloth had torn away. Earth biologists had theorized that the Proteps might be a roughly parallel mammalian form, but Hiller could not seem to assimilate the idea that Sarko might be a female.

"You . . . you're not a male," he said, and felt foolish.

"I'm neither male nor female," Sarko snapped, "though I'd hardly expect you to comprehend that."

"Get up," Hiller said. Sarko stood, tugging ineffectively at the torn fabric in an attempt to cover his chest.

"There will be a dozen guards at that door in seconds," he muttered. "What will you do then?"

Hiller was at him in one long step, his fingers closing around the throat. "I don't know if you have a hyoid bone in that scrawny neck or not, but I'm betting I could crush whatever passes for your windpipe in less time than it would take you to roll your eyes."

"You would actually kill me?" the alien said, aghast. There was a clatter in the hallway and the large door burst inward. Hiller tightened his grip. "Stop! I command it!" Sarko shrieked. Several Proteps dressed like Sarko halted in the doorway as others piled up behind them.

"Get away from the door," Hiller said. The guards backed away. Hiller jerked the alien's head around so that their faces were inches apart. "Your friends have no doubt captured Ilise by now, and I'm betting that they've brought her here, to the citadel. I want her in this room in five minutes."

"Impossible."

Hiller's fingers sank into the soft flesh of Sarko's neck. The inquisitor babbled something in his own tongue and two of the guards outside the door disappeared from view. "They are bringing her now," he wheezed. Anne laid a hand on Hiller's arm.

"Who . . . ?"

"I'll explain later."

In less than five minutes, they had brought her. She walked a bit unsteadily into the room, and Hiller could see the dullness of drugs in her eyes.

"'Lo, Hiller," she said thickly. "See they got you." Hiller motioned and Anne stepped forward and took the other woman in tow.

"Now we are going out that door," Hiller said. "The four of us. My hand stays on your neck. If someone plays the hero and shoots me, the nerve impulse in this arm will survive us both. Explain that to your goons." They stepped into the corridor, the silent group of Proteps falling back in front of them. Sarko babbled at them; they turned and scurried out of sight into side corridors. Hiller waited until their footsteps had faded in the distance, then gave Sarko's neck a firm squeeze. "Now you will lead us out of the citadel and into the countryside. I hope the word has been spread about your predicament; it would be a shame if anyone interfered."

"This is monstrous," Sarko huffed. "To think that you would damage—even kill me. . . ."

"You seemed to have no compunctions about us," Anne said.

"S'right," Ilise agreed sleepily.

"I did not damage you; you experienced pain, a subjective stimulus, but it was necessary. . . ."

"Just shut up and lead the way," Hiller snapped. Sarko trembled slightly but moved forward and the three humans followed. They wound through a labyrinth of featureless marblelike hallways for a while, with no sign of other Proteps. Then they descended into a smooth vertical cylinder, floating downward on a flat disc. After a short drop, they stepped off into a straight corridor which gleamed into the far distance. It was deserted.

"This way," Sarko muttered, and they set off. After walking in silence for about twenty minutes, Ilise's shuffling gait began to steady as she shook off the drugged lethargy.

"Why did you get me out?" she asked suddenly.

"It was the least I could do," Hiller said, glancing at her briefly.

She nodded. "You wish to make amends for forcing me to help you and then reporting me." She turned to Anne. "You are the spy?" Hiller cut off Anne's reply with a sharp glance.

"I found this woman strolling outside an estate and forced her to hide and feed me." A relieved look passed across Ilise's face; Hiller shrugged mentally, but felt disappointment. If she wanted to play it that way, he owed it to her to play along, but it meant he could not depend on her for more help or information. He was thinking about forcing the issue when they reached a pair of large doors and Sarko stopped.

"You asked to be taken to the countryside," he said. "It is out there. Enjoy it while you can." Hiller studied the alien.

"No doubt a number of your friends are waiting to greet us."

Sarko bristled. "Certainly not. I am not a fool, especially where my life is concerned. I have commanded that we not be followed or interfered with in any way. You are free to make your escape; I merely meant that your freedom will not last—we will find you again, Hiller."

"You expect me to believe that there is no ambush waiting for us the moment I release you?"

"I am not a treacherous Earth animal who knows nothing of honor." The alien spat the words and then shrank back as Hiller tightened his grip. Ilise laid a hand on his arm.

"What he says will be true," she said. "They keep their word."

"That is sensible of you, young woman," Sarko said. "Perhaps you may yet redeem yourself. After all, if you were truly forced by this savage . . ."

"Quiet," Hiller said. He looked at Anne; her meditative expression vanished and she shook her head.

"I don't trust him."

Hiller nodded and turned back to the alien. "After you."

Sarko stepped forward, Hiller's hand still making a yoke on his neck, and pulled the double doors inward, admitting a breeze which ruffled vines growing around the doorway. A grassy slope fell away to a lake shore backed by a brashery stand. They stepped out and looked around.

"What is this place?" Hiller asked. "Why should a tunnel be built from the citadel out here? There's no sign of anything."

"Shall I explain my whole culture to you in a word?" Sarko sneered. "There are many such tunnels, because it pleases us sometimes to walk in them. I have brought you to your freedom as you demanded; now let me go. My clothes are torn—I have no communication device; I must return through the tunnel before I can contact my forces. That will give you an adequate start."

"We'll walk to the woods together. Then, if I see no signs of treachery, I'll let you go." Sarko started immediately down the blue slope and the humans followed in silence, skirting the edge of the lake and reaching the brashery without incident. Ilise stopped first.

"You go on," she said to Hiller. "I am going back with Sarko."

"Don't be a fool. . . ."

"That is, I'll go back if he promises that I'll be exonerated and given my freedom."

"Why should I do such a thing?" Sarko said icily.

"It seems to me that I have proven my loyalty. After all, if I were a traitor to Eridani, I would choose to go with them. I'm sure they would like to learn what I could tell them of our society." Hiller noted the way Sarko stiffened at what seemed like a mild threat.

"Very well."

Hiller took Ilise's arm, but she shoved him away before he could say anything. "You've caused me enough trouble."

Hiller frowned. Had she winked at him?

"All right, get going."

Sarko turned and then paused. "I must warn you, Hiller; do not try to return to the transmitter, wherever you have hidden it. If you are able to reach it before you are recaptured, I must urge you not to use it. Only harm can come to you and your people if you do."

"I prefer to let the high command evaluate your prophecies," Hiller said. Let them sweat about the transmitter—it would take some of the heat off him. Sarko shook his head and set off quickly, followed by Ilise. When they had disappeared back into the tunnel, Hiller turned to find Anne watching him.

"How did you force her?" she asked.

"What? Oh." Hiller smiled. "By threatening to withhold my splendid body if she refused to help me."

"Hmph!" Anne snorted; but she moved possessively closer. "Don't you think you should read the note?"

"The note?" Hiller looked blank.

Anne laughed. "Some spy you are. The note Ilise shoved into your pocket just a few minutes ago, when she pushed you away. I saw her doing something with a piece of paper while we were in the tunnel; not writing, exactly. . . ."

Hiller fumbled at the pocket and withdrew a folded piece of material that felt like soft plastic. He opened it and his face went grim.

"Well? What does it say—meet me at the Five-Star Motel?"

Hiller handed her the note and the words began to fade as she read them aloud:

"The high council of Eridani meets very soon to decide on the destruction of Earth."

Twenty

Anne stared at Ilise's note, now blank, and blinked in surprise when more words began to form. Hiller took it from her fingers, which had begun to tremble slightly, and read the new words: NO CAN'T BE DON'T BELIEVE.

"It must receive words formed in your mind," he said, "and then convert them into script. When someone else looks at it, the message disappears and the sheet can form a new one. . . ." Anne's words began to fade and Hiller quickly folded the sheet and returned it to his pocket.

She groped for his hand. "Jared, we've got to get to your transmitter, warn Earth . . ."

"There isn't any transmitter."

"But Sarko . . ."

"They think I brought one with me. They apparently can't afford to think anything else. I encouraged him to believe it just now, because Proteps searching for the transmitter are not Proteps searching for us."

She studied him through narrowed eyes and pulled her hand away. "I get it. This is one of those things you think I'm better off not knowing. But what if something happens to you . . . ?"

"Damn it, I said there isn't any transmitter. . . ." He took a deep breath. "I'm sorry. I wish to God I did have one. . . ." He paused as the missing piece of information he'd tried to pull from his subconscious during Sarko's interrogation nagged at him again. Did it have something to do with the transmitter?

"Do you think they could really do it?"

Hiller rubbed his forehead in sudden weariness. "Probably. If they take Earth by surprise, almost certainly." He saw that she was still studying him. "You still don't believe me—about the transmitter."

"I'm sorry, Jad, I don't know. You try to protect me too much. . . ."

"Come on," he said gruffly. "We've got to get moving."

"Okay. Where?" Her voice sounded penitent.

"Right back to the city."

"But that's crazy. . . ."

"Exactly. The Proteps seem to have made a very thorough study of human logic, but that doesn't mean they understand our illogic. Kotyro said he would always get the better of me because he knows me. All right; let's do something I simply wouldn't do and see how well he knows me."

She nodded slowly. "Lead on."

There was a mound of grassy earth punctuated at intervals with surface ventilator ducts above the tunnel they had taken from the citadel. It was flanked on either side by rows of tall spreading treelike vegetation of a uniform cream color. It reminded Hiller of giant stalks of cauliflower; the contrast of them rising from the blue grass was startling, but Hiller was more interested in their potential as cover from aerial observation. He led the way at a trot, staying in the shade of the white trees and resting only when necessary. Before long they topped a rise and the city sprawled below. Hiller signaled a halt, settling onto his haunches and leaning back against one of the white trunks. Anne sank down beside him.

"Afraid I'm out of shape," she said between breaths. She looked out at the horizon where the sun was beginning to settle—a viridescent oval. Hiller wondered what element in the atmosphere could cause the light green color when the sun was close to the horizon. Perhaps a light nickel analogue combining with oxygen. . . .

"Are we going to wait for dark?"

He nodded. "We've got to get some different clothes, and a

small supply of food wouldn't hurt either. Then we'll try and find a hiding place where we can figure out our next move. . . ." He broke off as Anne cocked her head and raised a finger to her lips. A second later something whooshed by low overhead; then another and another.

"That makes you the ears of this outfit," Hiller whispered approvingly. "It appears Sarko has gotten back into hailing range."

"Oh, oh." Anne's face suddenly turned pale. "That makes me think of something. Do you remember when Sarko said 'my clothes are torn; I've got to go back through the tunnel before I can call my forces,' or something like that?"

Hiller nodded and frowned as her suspicion began to sink in.

"Well, maybe that means his suit was wired for communications or something," she said. "I've wired myself for sneak interviews enough times to suspect something like that. The trouble is, I'm wearing one of their suits."

Hiller adjusted the right eye and groaned as a webwork of fine wires popped into focus under the tan material. "You're right. Take it off—quick." But she was already shrugging out of the suit. Hiller looked around until his eyes fell on one of the metal ventilation ducts which stuck up at regular intervals along the outside of the tunnel. He grabbed the suit and searched through it until he found a tiny disc near the throat-piece which glowed with self-contained energy. Tearing it out, he ran to the duct and dropped it inside, trying to land it on the ceiling grill without it rolling through. Then he ducked back under the tree. "I doubt they could put a tracker on it now," he said, "and if they'd already picked it up, we wouldn't be standing here."

"Is it safe to put the suit back on?"

He gazed at her body. "Probably safer than leaving it off."

"Is there ever a time when you're not obsessed with sex?" She pulled the suit on with slow teasing movements.

"For about an hour afterwards."

"It must be awful to be at the mercy of your raging hormones."

"Umhmmm."

In another half hour the sun had set, leaving a breathtaking emerald afterglow, and Hiller had outlined most of what had happened since they were last together. No more craft had flown over and the trees around them were silent.

"It's a beautiful place," Anne sighed, nestling against him.

Hiller nodded. "When they came back and caught you standing by the vault shaft . . ."

"I left you my knife." She looked away, her face a cold silhouette. "Somehow, I knew you wouldn't die in there. They got me back to the hopter after the explosion and gave me a big dose of something. I didn't wake up until we were on Eridani. . . ." He felt her shudder.

"And you'd rather not talk about it."

She nodded.

They waited until only a little light remained, then Hiller stood and pulled her up after him. "Let's go shopping."

"What if they don't have stores on Eridani?"

Hiller searched for an answer and shrugged in the darkness when he couldn't find one. In another few minutes they were at the edge of a pool of light cast by the same type of floating discs Hiller had seen hovering over the estate lawn party. The discs were arranged in concentric rings over the circular domain of the city, the innermost ones lighting up the gleaming dome of the citadel, which brooded in the distance over the city.

"Act like you own the place," Hiller said. "Just stroll along and concentrate on looking like a part of the scene, whatever it turns out to be."

"Don't be nervous, Hiller," she said gently.

He chuckled. "Got my number, have you?"

They stepped into the light and were quickly among the first low fringe of buildings, which appeared to be homes. Hiller caught a whiff of the mint-scented intoxicant as they rounded the corner of a dwelling and saw a number of Proteps playing what looked like a complicated game of catch with a small golden cube. They were stripped to the waist and were hopping about animatedly, totally absorbed in the game. There were a few human faces on the edge of a crowd of onlookers and laughter mingled with the hoarse grunts of the aliens. One of the humans turned as they were passing, stared at them, and waved uncertainly. Hiller smiled and waved back. The fellow called out to him, but Hiller pointed at Anne and motioned him off. Hiller could feel the touch of the man's gaze along the nerves in his neck as they continued on their way. Then they rounded another corner and the cries fell off behind them.

"That smell," Anne said. "Is it the stuff you've talked about?"

Hiller nodded. "They seem to use it all the time. My guess is it's addictive."

They walked down a curving grassy mall between low structures which were set at apparently random angles to one another, as though variety had been the chief concern of the designers. The buildings were windowless and doorless, rounded at the top like inverted U's, and colored in rippling pastel hues that changed continually. There was nothing underfoot but the lush blue grass from which more of the white trees grew at irregular intervals. As they cut across several more malls, winding their way between the buildings, it became clear that the city was laid out either in a spiral or in concentric rings matching the pattern of light discs above. They saw only a few more Proteps and were able to avoid them without attracting attention. Finally, after they had covered about half the distance inward to the citadel, Hiller stopped between two of the buildings.

"All right, let's try a few of these. I don't want to be standing around in this jump suit when morning comes, and you can be sure that Sarko has issued a description of that lovely thing you're wearing."

Anne looked around hopelessly. "But there aren't any doors."

Hiller ran his hand along the wall next to him and stopped when his fingers disappeared part way into the smooth material. "In here."

Anne blinked. "Wait a minute; what if somebody's inside?"

"Then I'll curtsy out and we get away fast. Wait outside; if it's safe to come in, I'll stick my hand out."

Hiller stepped through and was met by the cloying odor of mint. He glimpsed a circle of inert rapturous faces before backing out quickly. He put a hand on Anne's shoulder and giggled.

"Jad?" She caught a whiff of his clothes, reached up and slapped him, hard. He shook his head and probed tenderly at his jaw.

"That's fine, but next time take off the steel gloves."

"What was it, a dope party or something?"

"They weren't singing hymns. Let's go somewhere else and try again." They visited two more buildings, both deserted, before they found the clothing place. Hiller stuck his hand back through the wall and Anne joined him. "May I present for the lady's pleasure and amusement the latest in summer design," he said with a sweeping gesture.

"What makes you think it's summer?" She looked around at the selection of bright gowns, robes, and other clothing. Each article or ensemble occupied a place of its own, draped over rounded display units. "Looks like no one's invented hangers here," she said, fingering a satiny gown that glowed under her touch like a Kirlian photograph.

"It goes along with the impressions I've gotten so far," Hiller said. "They know about hangers from their contacts with Earth; they just don't need them here—space is cheap, both actually and psychologically. These buildings, the layout of the city—everything indicates that there is more than enough room for everything and everyone."

She looked at him thoughtfully. "Or, putting it another way, not very many people for the amount of space."

"Exactly. They appear to be as undercrowded here as we are overpopulated on Earth. That can mean one of two things." Hiller watched as she slipped out of the tan suit and pulled on a co-ordinated outfit consisting of very short shorts and a high-necked, full-sleeved top of semisheer green material. She modeled it for him.

"Stunning," he said, "but I wonder if it will attract attention."

"It should," she said, "to my legs."

Hiller nodded. "And away from your face. That's good."

She frowned. "Was that a snide remark?"

"Look at it this way," Hiller said as he searched for something he could wear. "It probably won't make much difference to the Proteps—beauty being in the eye, and all that—but humans are humans, and Sarko is more likely to circulate a picture of your face than of your legs." He found a pair of loose-fitting dark trousers and a yellow toga top with elbow-length sleeves; topped it off with a skullcap that hid his red hair. "Grab as much as you can carry comfortably," he told her. "It won't do to have them simply changing the description of what we're wearing, based on what's missing." He gathered up several more outfits and then examined himself in a mirror. The skullcap helped considerably, but the eyes could still be a tip-off, especially with the thick copper-colored brows. "Have you seen anything like sunglasses here?" he asked.

Anne waved him over and handed him a pair of clear ones that wrapped around on the sides. He held them up to the light and they darkened immediately. "Good. You take a pair too." She tried on several, studying herself critically in the mirror.

"You said that the undercrowding could mean two things."

"I thought you'd never ask! All right, one: it could indicate that a combination of factors such as low birth rate, high death rate, population control, etc., have kept the population growth down. Two: the Proteps may be bleeding off excess population to colonize other worlds, exactly as Earth has been hoping to do these past twenty years or so."

"I like that second theory. It makes sense, given the Proteps' obvious capacity for rapid interstellar travel." Hiller looked at her thoughtfully.

"There's a problem with that, though. When I got off the ship from Earth, I had a chance to look around the spaceport and there was a good-sized fleet of ships tucked away to the side of the port. They were clearly survey and exploration ships and, just as clearly, most of them had never been used."

"Maybe some new development made them obsolete before they could be launched."

"Maybe. I don't have my chronometer up here, but from what I've seen so far, I doubt if there's been a new development around here in centuries."

"Why do you say that?"

"Call it a feeling. . . ." His eyes grew distant and Anne watched him for a moment. She laid a hand on his arm.

"You're thinking about the note?"

He nodded. "It's strange. For most of my life I've wanted to be off Earth—away from the crowding, the violence, what I regarded as the mass stupidity of people—and I've managed to do it. Then I had to live there with no hope of going off on the next mission and I hated it more. But from here it looks different. Sure, they're a mob—until you take them one by one. Then you find a lot of people like yourself, who want only what you want—a chance to stop scratching just to stay alive, a shot at getting far enough apart to be able to like one another. And now, just as it has become possible due to the Opperman drives, we're going to lose. The next quantum jump of the human race isn't going to happen as scheduled due to the end of the world. I'm trying, but I can't seem to take it in. . . ." His voice trailed off.

"Maybe it won't happen; maybe the note is wrong."

"I want to believe that, but I can't. There's a key to all of it somewhere. I've got some pieces of the puzzle but I can't see the pattern. Suddenly, after centuries of covert contact with the human race, they want to destroy us. It has to do with the underground vault, I'm sure. . . ."

"Wait a minute. What do you mean centuries? Did you find evidence of the Proteps in the vault?" Her face had gone pale.

"Not directly. The mummy was human, and so was everything else as far as I could tell, but there's got to be a connection. Otherwise, why would they be so anxious that no one on Earth discover the existence of the vaults?"

Anne shook her head. "Jad, we just don't have enough data."

"Maybe, but we've got to try. The note said 'very soon'; we've got to put this together and confront that council with something besides our bare faces, or . . ." Hiller's jaw stayed open; he stared past Anne to the place at the wall where they had entered—to the place where a tall Protep stood watching them.

Twenty-one

The alien said something in a mild voice. Hiller controlled the impulse to break for the door, patted Anne's hand, which had dug into his arm, and nodded. The Protep turned his attention to Anne and appeared to study her clothing, ending up, to Hiller's surprise, with a leisurely inspection of her legs. He said something else, apparently to Anne; she smiled and inclined her head, playing it as a compliment. The alien appeared satisfied. He gestured at the displays around him, talking animatedly and walking around the room. Hiller edged toward the entry place, keeping Anne's hand on his arm. When the Protep discovered their discarded clothes, he would have little trouble guessing who they were. The alien was still babbling over this and that article of clothing and Hiller was wondering if he was the Protep variant of the possibly universal salesman life form when the word "English" popped suddenly into the flow of his conversation. So the Protep had been close enough to overhear at least a few words. Hiller wondered briefly if there was such a thing as a Protep who did not know English. The alien had stopped talking and was peering at them with an expectancy bordering on suspicion, when Anne took over smoothly.

"Our services may soon be needed again as infiltrators; we are under strict instructions to speak nothing else but English and to avoid conversation in our own language. Please excuse us." Hiller held his breath as they walked toward the exit place. The alien called out after them and Anne turned, ignoring Hiller's tug on her arm. Reluctantly Hiller also looked back and saw that the Protep was holding out their discarded clothes. Anne walked over and took them with a cool thank-you. The Protep nodded.

"Let Oxo smile on your mission," he said. "Do not be caught in the destruction." Then it was Hiller's feet that hesitated and Anne had to pull his arm to get him outside.

"What's the rush," he said under his breath. "We could have pumped him for information."

She shook her head. "You're a very smart person, Hiller, but sometimes you surprise me. How would it look for us to quiz some Protep shopkeeper about things we should know, while he stands there remembering about a tan suit and two escaped human spies?"

Hiller nodded grudgingly. "Interesting that he expected no payment. There's probably so much of everything that rules of supply and demand don't operate here. Maybe everyone does their own thing with wholesale trading implicit in the arrangement." They cut across more of the malls, still working their way toward the citadel, while Hiller reviewed the encounter. "I wonder why the Protep didn't light up like a 'tilt' sign when he found our clothes?" he said after a while.

"Who knows. Maybe he doesn't listen to the radio, or whatever it is they listen to up here."

"The ComWeb. Maybe he doesn't, but that leaves you wondering how he knew that Earth is scheduled for demolition. Besides, unless I miss my guess, we should be about the hottest gossip on the planet right now."

She shrugged. "Maybe we're just lucky. We don't know how things work up here. I guess the trick is to stay loose and play everything by ear."

They stopped in the shadows next to a building bigger than any they'd passed so far. "I wonder what's in there," Hiller said, gazing up at the three-story expanse of wall.

"Now is hardly the time for exploring. We've got to put some distance between us and that shopkeeper." He nodded and they started to move on when a shout from the direction they had come halted them. Several answering shouts followed, each drawing closer to them. Anne gripped his arm. "We've got to run. . . ."

"No. We're going inside. Help me find the entrance." Placing his palms against the wall he hurried along its length. Glancing at the mall, Anne raced to the other end and began working toward him. The shouts were quite distinct now; Hiller could feel his heart thumping as he pressed against the wall, prodding for a hidden entrance portal.

"Over here," Anne whispered. He slid along the wall to join her. Just as several figures ran onto the mall, they slipped through into cool darkness and silence.

"Damn it, I can't see a thing."

Hiller took her hand. There was enough light for his right eye to make out a high arched ceiling and a long chamber flanked on either side by what looked like ranks of glasite panels.

"Come on," he whispered. "There seem to be nooks along the side." They moved into the middle of the room, their footfalls slapping back from the ceiling despite their efforts to walk softly.

"I wish we had lights," Anne complained, and instantly the chamber was flooded with painful brilliance.

"Lights off," Hiller countered instantly, and the room plunged once more into darkness.

"Now I'm really blind."

"In here." Hiller pulled her into a small hallway as the lights came on again. Voices echoed back and forth and broke into mocking ripples. Then there was silence except for the sound of footsteps, which seemed to come from everywhere at once. Hiller looked around quickly and saw that they were trapped in a short cul-de-sac, with no visible doors. A quick turn up and back, with his hands brushing the walls, revealed no hidden exits either. Spying a pile of padded material shoved into a back corner of the hallway, he motioned Anne toward it, holding up the edge. She burrowed in, groping ahead with her hands as he followed, trying not to choke on the dusty air. After a moment he felt rather than heard the footsteps entering the hallway. They came up to the padding, vibrating through the floor into his back, and stopped. Sweat rolled into Hiller's eyes and mingled with the grime from the covering. A foot kicked the padding; then steps receded until he could no longer feel any footfalls through the floor. They waited a few moments before throwing back the heavy padding and tiptoeing to the door of the hall.

"They've gone," Hiller said. "I can't believe he didn't look under the padding."

"They're not very thorough," Anne agreed. "It appears that our shopkeeper friend listens to the ComWeb after all."

"And has a thirty-minute reaction time." Hiller stepped into the chamber. "Let's look around."

Anne hung back. "Jad, as soon as Sarko knows we came back into the city, he'll be combing it for us. It was a nice plan while it lasted, but we've got to get out to the countryside again, where we stand a chance."

"I don't think so—the Proteps have a taboo against invading private dwellings. That puts at least the homes in this city out of Sarko's reach, so there's not much point to searching the rest of it. The best thing for him to do is cordon off the city and wait for us to make a break for it."

"But do we have to stay here? I don't know why, but this place frightens me."

"Going outside again scares me worse," Hiller answered. "Besides, if it comes down to a search, they've already been here. Can we have some dim lights please. . . ."

The central chamber lit up with a diffuse glow. Anne shook her head, but joined Hiller as he inspected one of the glass-type panels he'd noticed when they came in. Behind it was a display case, now also lit, which contained crude axes and other implements made with wood and stone and secured with strips of hide. On most of the weapons the blades gleamed like newly chipped stone. None of the implements showed signs of age—they had not been excavated from some buried ruin but were preserved in newly minted condition. Hiller's eyes swept quickly around the rest of the chamber; both of the long walls were lined with displays.

"A museum," Anne said.

"And those are tools from one of the early eras."

"Parallel evolution?"

"I don't think so." Hiller pushed a button set into a panel beside the case and an alien voice began to narrate. It took Hiller a moment to realize that the sound was not coming from any direction, but seemed to be produced entirely inside his head. He looked at Anne; her face was screwed into a frown and she had covered both ears with her hands.

"Jared, I. . . ." The alien's voice cut off when she spoke and she dropped her hands.

"Just a gimmick," he said. "They've evidently found a way to directly stimulate the inner ear. Did you catch the words on the tape?"

"You mean the English ones—Stone Age . . ."

"Exactly. If this stuff was really from Eridani's past, why would they use the words 'Stone Age'?"

"Maybe they were just making comparisons."

Hiller looked skeptical and motioned her on to the next display, a full-size, waxlike model of a man, covered with coarse black hair. The rendering was exact; the eyes stared out from beneath shaggy brows in a lifelike frown. Hiller punched the button and waited until he heard the word 'Neanderthal' before shutting off the commentary.

"He looks so real," Anne whispered. "As though someone actually sneaked up on him while he was out hunting and froze him where he stood."

Hiller nodded. It was as though one last image was sealed into the wax eyes—a tall, blue-skinned figure and perhaps in the background a space ship. . . .

"I told you this place was creepy. Can't we go somewhere else?"

Hiller moved on as though he had not heard and she followed glumly past more displays of Earth artifacts spanning the full range of early man. The cases were arranged in chronological order into the past and Hiller pushed by them—past *Homo erectus,* past the ape-like Ramapithecus, to the end of the hall. There he found it, in the last display case. Anne joined him and drew in her breath. The man stood about six feet eight inches tall, with firm muscles filling out the skin-tight suit of iridescent colors. The forehead was high and the eyes set by the artist into a look of calm intelligence. In the background was portrayed a city skyline like the one Hiller had seen on the screen in the underground vault on Earth.

"Looks like they got this one out of order," Anne said after a moment. Hiller shook his head but did not answer. He was thinking about the mummy in the vault medical section that was twelve million years old, of the clouds of red gas descending from wingless craft, and of the reasons why a city might be built three hundred yards underground.

"Jad . . . ?"

"I've got to think," he muttered. He left her standing and walked past the displays along the other wall—exotic scenes and artifacts, this time of Protep origin. Hiller looked at them as he passed but they hardly registered. It all seemed much clearer now, but something still wasn't right—there was too much that didn't make sense. Anne caught up with him.

"Jad, let's get out of here. If someone walks through that door . . ."

He nodded and was about to turn away from the displays when he noticed an arched doorway several windows down where a case should have been. Taking Anne's hand, he walked through into a round room draped with purple curtains. The walls stretched upward like the shaft of a castle tower to where a skylight framed the smaller of Eridani's two moons.

It was the dais in the center of the room that captured their attention, though. There, suspended in amber fluid in a crystal bubble, was the preserved body of a human child.

Twenty-two

They stared at it for a long time without speaking. After a moment, Hiller thought he saw it lift one arm slightly in the yellow fluid; he looked away.

"Why?" Anne said at last.

Hiller shook his head. "Why are things usually put in museums?"

He walked closer to the dais and looked at the alien inscription around the base. There were no English words and no button to push for commentary.

"You mean . . ."

"To preserve the memory after something's gone," Hiller said softly.

"That doesn't make sense, unless they've been planning for a long time to destroy us—this exhibit looks fairly old. Maybe this is just meant to show the average Protep who has never been on Earth what a human child looks like." She shuddered.

"Maybe. But why put it off here in a separate room? Why preserve a real body instead of simply making a model?" He stepped to the dais and examined the child more closely. It was a perfectly formed female with russet hair and wide blue eyes that stared at them through the fluid bath. There was no wound on it and no sign of disease.

"It's so lovely . . . so sad. . . ." Anne's voice caught and Hiller saw a glistening path down her cheek. He put an arm around her and turned her gently away from the dais. She leaned against him for a few moments, then looked up the shaft of the tower.

"The moon is gone now," she said, and her voice was calm.

"Yes."

She looked back at the child. "First everyone on Earth, then, one by one, the people they've retired up here. Maybe they'll take a pair of them before they grow old and put one on either side of her: Human reproductive unit—Adult Male, Adult Female, Female Pup. Jad, maybe it'll even be you and me. . . ."

"Stop it."

"That's why they've got this museum with one whole wall devoted to the human race—they knew that we were going to become extinct. . . ."

Hiller gripped her arm and she stopped, arrested by the look of excitement in his eyes.

"That's it!" he exclaimed, wondering how the idea could have eluded him for so long. "Let's go."

"What's got into you? Go where?"

"To the transmitter."

She pulled him to a stop. "I knew it! I knew you were lying. Where is it?"

Hiller set off walking again and she followed to where they had first entered the museum. "I wasn't lying. I didn't bring a transmitter, but one might exist not three miles from here."

"I don't understand. . . ."

"Remember I told you about the captured ship at the spaceport—the *Hound*?"

She nodded, then her face lit in comprehension. "Do you mean there's a transmitter on the ship?"

"There might be. They were first beginning to install transmitters at the time the *Hound* was launched. Naturally I was not briefed on the *Hound's* mission or equipment, but I'm betting it's there. The transmitters are installed as an integral part of the ship's circuitry, so it would be hard to detect; besides, Kotyro referred to the transmitters as being small, which means that the Proteps didn't discover the one on the *Hound*—if it's there."

Anne nodded. "What are we waiting for?"

They stepped through the portal and found the mall deserted. After working their way in silence for a while back toward the edge of the city, Hiller stopped.

"The place seems deserted," he whispered. "It's giving me bad feelings."

Anne shrugged. "Maybe everyone goes to bed early around here."

"I hope that's all it is."

They moved on into the last fringe of buildings before the grassy slopes that surrounded the city. The iridescent lights that had painted the sides of the dwellings earlier had vanished and the light discs above were dimmer, leaving dark passages between the buildings.

"Are you sure we're going in the right direction?"

Hiller consulted his mental copy of the map Ilise had shown him. "Yes. The spaceport should be about two miles that way." Slipping down an alley between two houses, Hiller examined the slopes and was about to step out when a sixth sense warned him. He motioned Anne back and flattened himself against the wall, edging toward the corner of the building. Holding his breath, he listened; a foot swished in the grass and clothing rustled softly as someone shifted positions. He backed away, leading Anne around to the inner exposure of the house. "We've got to get out of sight, quick," he whispered. "There's a reception party back of the house; they may have heard us coming."

She looked around. "But where can we go?"

He edged along the front of the dwelling, feeling for the entry portal.

"Jad, we can't just—"

He cut her off with a sharp motion and disappeared halfway into the wall, waving at her to follow. His face barely emerged from the inside of the portal when it jolted against a metal door. He stopped in surprise, felt Anne's hand on his back, and groped for the knob, twisting. The lock was good; it held for a full two seconds before popping. The door yielded inward and Anne stumbled through on his heels.

There was a light on; Hiller's eyes snapped up a few details of the room before locking on the cowled and robed figure against the far wall.

"Please do nothing rash, or I will be forced to shoot you." The words came muffled through the black mask; Hiller's mind flashed back to the alien craft which had deposited a number of similarly clothed and masked figures into the underground chamber in the newly cleared space of the brashery stand. The shoulders under the robe were broader than any Protep's but the hand that held the tubelike weapon was light blue.

"Take it easy," Hiller said, raising his hands.

"You take it easy, Mr. Hiller. This weapon kills. Sarko will be glad to get you back."

"I don't think so," Hiller said. He began to edge toward the figure.

"I warned you. . . ."

"I know. You warned me that the weapon kills. What will Sarko do to you, do you think, if you kill me? I'm sure he still has some questions he'd like to ask me." Hiller was ten feet away now. The tube wavered downward.

"I could shoot you in the leg. . . ."

"And risk my bleeding to death? We humans are quite fragile, you know." The distance had shrunk to five feet and the figure pressed backward against the wall. Hiller's throat tightened and the blood pounded in his ears.

"All right. Just go. I won't shoot."

"Jad, let's get out of here."

"Not yet." Hiller's hand lashed out and knocked the tube across the room. The figure tried to run, but Hiller caught him; they grappled and fell to the floor, rolling over and over. Hiller came out on top and pinned the creature's arms to the floor with his knees and one hand. With the other he grasped the mask and tore it off.

Twenty-three

The face that stared back at him was human—almost. The features, the shape of the skull, and the shallow eye sockets were right, but the face was light blue and hairless. The jaw was narrower than any human jaw he'd seen, but still broader than a Protep's. He felt Anne move up beside him; heard her gasp.

"It . . . it's a cross between a Protep and a human—a hybrid. Look out!" The creature gave a convulsive heave, half throwing Hiller off, as something clattered at the door. Hiller sprang upward to meet the new threat. There were two of them; he had just enough time to see that they were human before they were on him, moving with the silent speed of trained guard dogs. Hiller took the brunt of a blow along his upraised right arm and let himself tumble backward, tangling his legs with theirs. The three of them went down together as the hybrid scurried off into a side room. Hiller was up first, shooting his elbow hard against the skull of one man. The other hit him under the ribs with something solid; he caught a glimpse of Anne's white face before he went down gasping. The man followed up with a kick, then stiffened and pitched forward over Hiller, revealing Anne behind, with one hand raised. She rubbed the edge of her little finger as Hiller struggled up and caught his breath.

"Thanks."

"I never hit anyone exactly like that before. It hurts." She nursed the swelling finger. Hiller grabbed the mask that he'd torn off the hybrid's face and ransacked the room until he found a closet cubicle with more masks and several cowled robes.

"We'd better hurry," Anne said. "There are beginning to be noises outside." Hiller tossed her a robe and mask.

"Time for another identity change." The robes were big on Anne and small on Hiller, but the masks molded themselves to their faces as soon as they put them on.

"Let's go."

They ran out of the alley together as houses around them lit up and the floating discs flared into brilliance. Hiller expected more assailants, but the slope was clear. By the time the clamor was at full pitch behind them, they had gained the protection of the brashery stand and soon lost the sound among the cushioning trunks. Hiller thought hard as he ran, trying to digest the new datum: Why was it so important to conceal the identity of the hybrid creatures beneath masks, in underground warrens, and behind locked doors—which were otherwise nonexistent on Eridani? He sensed that the answer might be the final piece he had been searching for, to make sense of the whole puzzle, but still it eluded him. They moved on quickly for a while, Anne stumbling through the blackness with a hand on Hiller's back; then he stopped and she bumped against him.

"We're not far away, now," he whispered. "The storage pads are just ahead—past those bushes."

"I'm glad someone can see."

Hiller led her through and onto the pads. Eridani's second moon peeked over the treetops and spilled blue light onto the field, painting the ranks of deserted ships in tombstone hues.

Anne shivered against him. "It's eerie. . . ."

Hiller nodded. "There's the *Hound*. Let's see if our luck holds." He started forward and then stopped.

"What's the matter?"

"Just thinking about luck. Does it strike you that we've been almost too lucky?"

"What do you mean?"

"Getting away from Sarko and his crew, avoiding capture in the city, getting away just now. . . ."

"That shopkeeper is still bothering you—the one who didn't turn in the alarm for half an hour."

"Not just that. When we were in the citadel and Sarko brought me to where they were keeping you, none of the Proteps were armed—it's almost as if they wanted me to escape. Then, after we got away, we practically marched into the middle of their city without being caught. And the pads, here; why aren't they guarded? They know we're loose and that I may well have seen the *Hound;* yet there it stands just waiting for us."

Anne peered at the leaning hulk—at the hole in the side where the drives were located. "I think you're being paranoid. Why should they guard it? They evidently don't realize that there might be a transmitter aboard—Kotyro's description proves that—and the drives are clearly useless."

Hiller started to reply and in that instant everything fell into place; he knew why Stanek hadn't aged in twenty-five years, why the Proteps were hunting down the underground vaults on Earth, why they meant to destroy the planet—all that and much more besides. He felt first exultation and then despair. Anne was watching him intently.

"Let's give it a try," he said.

The layout of the *Hound* was similar to that of his own ill-fated *Trojan,* and he felt a surge of conflicting emotions as he led Anne through a narrow passage to the bridge ladder. What had they done with the crew, he wondered? Had Captain Ketterly, his soft-spoken friend who liked poetry and lunar cigars, died in the citadel, his brain refusing to fight on through the endless pain of Sarko's rod? Hiller suppressed the image and concentrated on climbing in the darkness through the familiar passages. When they reached the bridge, he took off his mask and the sweat-soaked robe and laid them over the open floor hatch. Then he groped for the emergency switch and the bridge was flooded with light. He walked to the elevated chair in the middle and sat down.

"It's been almost a year, hasn't it, Jad?" Her voice was soft.

"Yes." He got up again, self-consciously, and his eyes swept the tiny circular deck; engineer's station, science instruments, the exec's monitoring headset behind the captain's chair, and finally, the signals board. Walking over slowly, he put a hand on the back of the signal officer's seat. A small extra key on the board told him everything. The new narrow-beam transmitter was there. He felt no surprise.

The control and coding panels seemed intact; he played his fingers along the test keys and watched a sequence of lights wink. According to the feedback telltales, the transmitter was ready to send. He glanced at Anne, who was standing near the hatch. She had removed her mask; her forehead was creased with tension, but she smiled at him. He sat in the webbed chair and a minute passed while he stared at the board. Anne moved restlessly behind him; laid a hand on his shoulder.

"Just composing the message," he said. "Luckily there's no need to encode the words, themselves, since they're going in on a tight-coded beam to Allied Control and nowhere else." He flicked a switch and the computer tie-in lit up. Then he thought about the spatial co-ordinates to the underground nerve plexus of the Alliance—the true power center of the planet Earth. The co-ordinates were a simple set of four three-digit code numbers known only to the high command, and to a handful of its agents; four numbers which his body would die to conceal, no matter what the frontal lobes of his brain wanted.

He pushed rapidly at the array of co-ordinate number keys: three stop, three stop, three stop, three stop. The computer chattered softly for a few seconds, analyzing an eleven light-year long tunnel of space between Earth and Eridani for the exactly proper route, compensating for planetary movement, adjusting a hundred other parameters. Then the screen lit up with the message "Locked in and Ready."

On an ordinary typewriter console Hiller tapped out, "AM AT LARGE ON ERIDANI. DESTRUCTION OF EARTH BY PROTEPS IMMINENT. COUNTERMEASURES REQUIRED SOONEST. MESSAGE SENT FROM CAPTURED A.S.N. SHIP HOUND. HILLER." After arranging for the computer to compress the message into repeating thirty-millisecond bursts, he punched the transmit button with the heel of his hand. Now he would have his answer. With a sigh, he settled back in the chair.

"Is that it?"

"That's it. It's up to Allied Command, now."

There was a silence which seemed long to Hiller and then she said, "I'm sorry, Jared. Truly sorry."

He turned and his eyes met hers for a long moment before dropping to the blaster in her hand.

Twenty-four

"Where did you get the blaster?" His voice was conversational.

"They left it for me under the science officer's charts."

Hiller looked at her and felt an almost physical weight pressing him into the chair. The transmitter had been dead. It was rigged to look operational so that he would give away the co-ordinates of Allied Command. Anne had betrayed him; if only he'd been wrong. He thrust his feelings aside; the scene must be played out properly.

"Did you ever suspect?"

"Does it matter?" Hiller knew very well that it did. She nodded. "All right then; no, I haven't. Oh, there've been things from time to time that made me wonder—the determined way you stuck to me after we'd first met, your combat abilities—you don't become skilled in half a dozen forms of mayhem with six years of lessons, let alone three. The synpape-reporter cover was good for that, though, and for the way you kept playing devil's advocate every time I got close to the truth. Of course, I didn't know it was the truth, then. Still, I should have suspected—at a dozen different points I should have suspected. They meant for me to get you out; that way you could give me gentle steers to the transmitter, if necessary. It was a beautiful setup. Kotyro pretending never to have seen one of our transmitters, acting like the worst thing I could do to them was send a message to Allied Command, when all along it was exactly what they wanted. How else could they get the co-ordinates. Of course, they couldn't be sure I'd seen the *Hound.* That was another reason you had to be along—to suggest that they might have one of our ships if I failed to come up with it." Hiller looked at the signals board. "I suppose the ship is surrounded."

"Yes." Her voice was barely audible.

"Well, shouldn't you be delivering me to them?"

"We have time. They'll wait until I call."

"Good. Reminiscing is such fun. That morning back on Earth when we woke up so late—too late to see Stanek and his boys cover the vault entrance and steal away—you make a mean cup of cafee, love, but you underestimated the dose a little, didn't you? Probably overcompensated for my reduced circulatory system. I was able to get a real eye—and photaper—full before the vault started disintegrating around my ears. I guess you must have called Stanek back, too, just to make sure I didn't get out alive. But one thing puzzles me; why did you leave the knife and drag your feet going out? Was it just a precaution in case the impossible happened and I survived?" When she said nothing he nodded approvingly. "Very thorough. It preserved your usefulness to the end."

"I never wanted you to die, and even though I got in trouble for it later, I didn't call Stanek back either; he came on his own. If you thought all this about me, why didn't you challenge me long ago?"

"Ah, but I didn't think it of you. That's the real clincher. I've known all of these things somewhere in my mind but I haven't really suspected you at all—not until now, when it's too late. There was always some innocent explanation; I wanted to believe in you, and you were good—really good. A lesser artist would have slipped up dozens of times instead of one or two, and even a lovesick navy officer would have been able to reason things out."

"Don't talk about love as a sickness," she said in a small voice.

"Isn't it?" Hiller gazed at her. "It seems to have been fatal for me—and for Earth. The whole thing was such a masterful charade. From the moment they knew I'd survived the explosion, stowed away and gotten loose on Eridani, they were thinking of ways to make it all pay off big, and you were the key actor. They knew they couldn't get the co-ordinates to Allied Command out of me by force—they probably tried it on the captain of the *Hound* and came up with a corpse. But they wanted those numbers; a vast technological edge isn't enough for them. If they can knock out Allied Command first, then the rest will be a cakewalk. Otherwise, it doesn't matter how many of the sheep they slaughter, there will still be the shepherds to deal with—one or two Proteps might even be killed." He turned and looked at the signals station. "I'll give your boys credit; they know their paratronics—fooling the telltales built into this baby is supposed to be impossible, and yet I was convinced that it was a live transmitter." Hiller got up and walked to the captain's chair, glancing only once at the way she held the blaster. "When is the base going to be hit?"

"As soon as the co-ordinates are decoded," she answered quietly. "Follow-up operations will commence as soon as we confirm destruction of Allied Command. Jad, it would be better if you would not think about it."

Hiller sank down at the conn and closed his eyes, overcome suddenly by terrible weariness. He sat like that for a time, sorting through the tangled thought-skeins while the ship seemed to float around him, suspended outside space and time. Anne did nothing to disturb the moment and at last he opened his eyes; studied her.

"Why did they do it—put you on me in the first place?"

"Because of your mission. You were right about York. He sabotaged the Opperman drives and exited through the lock. He was supposed to simply disable the drives so that you couldn't warp out, but something went wrong."

"Something went wrong. . . ." Hiller stood and began to pace, stopping after a moment to take a few calming breaths. "Where is York now?" His voice was too casual, he knew.

"Dead. He was supposed to cross over to the cruiser, in case there had to be shooting. When the *Trojan* blew up he was sliced in half by a fragment of hull."

A door closed in Hiller's mind. He sat down again.

"When the council learned that you survived there was an awful flap," she continued. "They didn't know what had happened on board—whether you were aware that York's signal was not accidental." Hiller nodded as her words brought back the buried memory of York, lying white-faced beside the norm-space transmitter. "For all they knew, you had caught him sabotaging the drives. It would be the first reason Earth had to suspect infiltration by human agents working for the Proteps. . . ."

"Just a minute. Why have York signal at all? You obviously knew we were coming and there can't be that many asteroid chunks falling into your atmosphere."

"We knew that you were sending another mission, but York had no chance before take-off to tell us about the disguise of your ship."

Hiller nodded. The security precautions had been extensive; only Allied Command had known about the outer design before boarding time, and they had not been infiltrated or the Proteps would have known the co-ordinates of the command center and he would not be sitting aboard the *Hound* at this moment.

"So the council found out I'd been picked up in my emergency belt sack, three-fourths dead, and brought back to Earth by the *Littlejohn.* Why didn't they just send in someone to finish the job?"

She hesitated. "Whether you will believe it or not, the council abhors unnecessary violence. They will use it only if no other solution is available."

"I'm impressed, especially since they now plan to exterminate the entire population of a planet."

She ignored his biting tone. "They decided to have you watched closely. At the hospital . . . and later."

"The nurse," Hiller murmured, remembering suddenly how solicitous the young woman had been—reading to him during the long convalescence, holding his one hand, listening to him struggle in futile rambling sessions to remember what had happened to him. And then Anne, picking him up a scant few weeks out of hospital. Without the two of them, he might still be lying in a clinic bed, half vegetable, or sitting perched on the edge of a rooftop bar, envying through an alcoholic haze those with the guts to jump. How ironic that his belief in their caring should have saved him. But was it ever any different, he wondered—did it matter why someone cared, as long as they cared?

"When Stanek showed up in the bar, I knew I had been jinxed," Anne said. "It was the first step in the trail that has ended here. If it hadn't been for his blundering, you wouldn't have discovered the vaults, we would not be here; Earth would not be on the brink . . . I tried to stop you; to deflect you at every turn—devil's advocate, you called it."

He looked up at her. "You should have stopped me. You could have slipped that blade of yours between my shoulders almost at any time."

"You don't mean that. . . ."

"Of course not. I'm much more important than the human race."

"I . . . I couldn't, anyway." She looked away and Hiller saw that her eyes were wet. "They chastened me for it in council—said my methods had been inadequate, indecisive. They said I should have poisoned you that night before the vaults, instead of just drugging you—that the time for sparing you passed the moment you got close to the vaults. We—they have a drug that mimics heart failure perfectly. Even Pierce would not have been suspicious. But they couldn't know how I felt. I couldn't let them know—I would have been instantly replaced and then I would have lost you for certain."

"How touching. . . ."

"Oh stop it, for God's sake, Hiller, will you please . . ." She stopped, drew a hand across her face. "Will you please try and understand? Once you discovered the vault, took pictures of it, told Pierce about it, everything was sealed. It was only a question of time. The council has feared that discovery most for all these . . . years."

"Centuries, you mean; you needn't try to hide any of it now—not now that it's too late. That was Stanek's job, wasn't it? Stanek's and a long line of infiltrators before him; to find the underground refuges of the first epoch of man and destroy every vestige of them—every trace of the knowledge and culture that could rekindle a feud wiped from the history of Earth twelve thousand *millenniums* ago, right about when the first prehuman strains were supposed to have broken off from the apes. I wonder what it was like before the great war with the Proteps—that first culture of man?"

"It was a hate-filled warren," Anne said with surprising vehemence, "just as it is today. Oh, it had its science, far greater than the simple technology to which Earthmen have so slowly returned. But it was a seething polluted hive, nonetheless."

"And the overlord government of the Proteps had to take increasingly harsh measures," Hiller said, "like trying to curb population with pogroms launched against entire cities." The image of the red gas descending from the wingless craft burned again into his mind. Anne inclined her head. "But it wasn't the answer then, either," he continued. "Earth needed growing room, not brutal containment. But there were no ships. With all its culture and science, Earth did not have an interstellar drive—not until nearly the end of the great civil war, when only a few underground cities remained."

"Civil war?" Anne's voice had gone low, and her eyes were locked on his.

"Yes. That was the real puzzler all along. Just what was the relationship between the Proteps and the humans? Where did the Proteps come from? How did they achieve their dominance and what has kept them bound psychologically to Earth through the eons since that first great destruction—so much so that fleets of space-going ships equipped to explore a thousand exotic worlds rot outside the ports and one planet alone claims their attention? It had me stumped right up to the last, until we broke into the house and I pulled the mask off that creature."

"You mean the hybrid?"

"That's what you wanted me to think; it was a clever improvisation. But why would the Proteps go to such great trouble, making a special underground compound for them as soon as they realized I was on the planet and then, after I had stumbled across it, installing special inner doors in houses where there was such a creature? And on top of it, there were masks and hoods as a final protection. Could it be merely to hide the product of a marriage between alien and human—no more nor less than a biologist's curiosity? When I realized what that creature really is, it solved everything. That's when I realized that it had been a *civil* war on Earth, not a conflict between two different species; that the Proteps didn't need to subvert disgruntled or vulnerable humans with promises of rejuvenated limbs or long lives in order to maintain their link with Earth."

"What are you saying?"

"You know what I'm saying." He gazed back at her until her eyes wavered and fell. "Among other things, I'm saying that you are not merely a spy for the Proteps. You are a Protep."

Twenty-five

"You," Hiller said, "Stanek and his friends, York, Ilise, and all the other people on this planet—all Proteps."

"I'm as human as you are."

"I never said you weren't. Let's not play word games—I know the truth now."

"So I'm a Protep, huh? What am I supposed to do, peel off my flesh-colored mask so that my blue pumpkin head can pop out?"

"No. Time will do that for you," Hiller said softly. "Won't it?"

She looked at him for a long time and then nodded.

Hiller pressed on. "Twelve million years ago the Proteps didn't come from some other planet to conquer Earth. They were—and are—human. Protep meant something different then; it meant only what words like ruler, overlord, governing class, and so on have meant in the subsequent eras of man." He paused. "The problems came with the advent of immortality drugs, didn't they? Until then there were only three indistinct but basic stages of human growth followed by a final stage of descent into death: Infancy, childhood, and adulthood, followed by old age, the way it still is on Earth. But the Proteps, who left Earth and journeyed across space to settle Eridani, brought with them a secret which permitted them to eliminate that unnatural fourth stage, death. Every Protep who embarked on that journey has since been free to realize his full genetic and developmental destiny. Just as the infant is quite different physically from the adult, the following stages continue to be different from each other. How long does it take before the hair begins to fall out, the skull starts to broaden, the eyes deepen? How long before the flesh turns blue . . . ?"

"About three hundred years," Anne said quietly. "It happens gradually over a period of about fifty years."

"And are there other stages after that?" Hiller felt excitement grow in him despite everything. It was an undreamed of idea—man reaching forever outward not through the capricious cycles of evolution, which continually gave life and then snatched it away, but through endless personal development of each individual mind and body!

"We have identified three more stages among our oldest members," she answered, "each of successively longer duration according to a roughly exponential progression."

An oddly chilling thought struck Hiller. "And you; how old are you?"

She returned his gaze levelly. "Two hundred and thirty-three Earth years." Hiller sucked in his breath; let it out again slowly. He studied her clear unwrinkled skin, the fine nose with its slight imperfection from the fracture.

"You don't look a day over one hundred," he said at last. She smiled but his face remained hard, rebuffing her.

"When were the drugs discovered?"

She looked at him, but her eyes were distant; communing. "It was ironic, really. The drugs were first synthesized by the ruling scientist class—the *Protepitet*—a few years before the civil war to which you so accurately referred. The last thing Earth needed then was a longevity drug, and the knowledge was carefully suppressed. Even so, the rumors leaked out that certain of the *Protepitet* were secretly taking immortality drugs even as they enforced stricter and stricter population control measures against the masses."

"So the peasants revolted?"

"It wasn't a question of peasants. The scientist class was divided on the question. Some argued that the formula should be destroyed and its memory erased from the minds of their colleagues who had discovered it. Others, particularly those who controlled the secret, saw this for the egalitarian nonsense it was —the same attempts to drag mankind to its lowest common denominator that noble-sounding pleas for equality have always disguised."

Hiller was surprised at her easy digression into elitist rhetoric. "You're reciting dogma."

"And what if I am?" she answered coolly. "There is always dogma—it remains only for us to choose. Anyway, why shouldn't the creators of the drug be entitled to reap the fruits of their genius? All of them renounced having any more children. Or do you believe that the inventors were obliged to die in order to accommodate the very offspring who would carry on the irresponsible birth policies that would ruin Earth?"

Hiller said nothing.

She took a deep breath and continued. "So it was some of the lesser *Protepitet* and most of the populace aligned against the upper *Protepitet* and their small following of soldiers and technicians. At some point during the war the scientists of the lesser *Protepitet* developed a process for perfectly shielding underground chambers from detection. They made a stand in these *Uluspansa* and the tide of the war turned. Immune from conventional counterattack, they hunted down the scattered forces of the upper *Protepitet,* whose only remaining tactical advantage of air superiority was effectively negated by the *Uluspansa.* In desperation, the upper *Protepitet* undertook a saturation air strike campaign using dirty radiation atomics and containers of a virulent bacterial strain." Anne's voice became low; her eyes focused on empty space. "Evidently the bacteria were carried by returning soldiers into the *Uluspansa.* There was plague and death, driving many back to the surface. It got out of hand; most of the upper *Protepitet* were infected, too. A small group in the mountains had been working on prototypes of a space vessel. When the plague spread out of control and a wayward air current brought radiation close to their hiding place, they knew they were out of time. Three hundred of them escaped from Earth in six huge ships with makeshift sublight drives. It took them over a hundred years to reach the Epsilon Eridani star system, but they had an ample supply of the longevity drug and breeding was strictly controlled."

"As it has been since?"

Her eyes focused on him. "Yes."

Hiller nodded to himself. "No more repetition of Earth's earlier folly."

"No." She seemed suddenly withdrawn.

"So, after two hundred more years, the first of you started turning blue and changing shape—I'll bet it came as a shock."

"I suppose; but it's all perfectly natural—no different than an adolescent growth spurt."

"You're looking forward to it, then?"

"Looking forward to it?" She smiled slowly and Hiller caught a glimpse of something, as though a door had opened and shut: A vast and penetrating intelligence—a wisdom which left him feeling small and naïve. He flushed; tried to pick up an earlier thought train. "All right, after your ancestors had been on Eridani awhile, they developed a faster-than-light drive and started keeping watch on Earth."

"The people were all savages," she said softly. "Only a few—apparently all children—had survived the bacteria and radiation, and the reversion to barbarism was complete. By the time we returned, most showed mutations of the skull and spinal areas. Your *Homo erectus* was an offshoot strain, as were all the rest. Not until Cro-Magnon man established himself a bare thirty-five thousand years ago did the truly human strain re-emerge. It was this slow breeding back to the original genetic template that misled your scientists in their theories of evolution. The true origins of man are lost in a greater antiquity than you have ever imagined."

Hiller shook his head slowly, trying to take it all in. "And always you watched us, waiting to see if we would ever be a threat again; wondering if the ancient blood feud would have its resurrection."

She nodded. "When Earth people began to mine and to drill for oil, we became afraid," she murmured. "Afraid that you would eventually stumble across one of the *Uluspansa*—that your archaeologists would then piece together the buried truths. We tried desperately from that point on to find a way of locating the chambers, but the secret of their shielding had died millenniums ago with those who invented it. Only in the last thirty years did we finally succeed in developing a detection device. . . ."

"Stanek's 'breadbox.'"

She nodded. "By then we were restricted, due to the increased numbers and sophistication of Earth's population, to covert operations with a limited force of agents. If only we'd anticipated the discovery and use of fossil fuels instead of fixed magnetics, we'd have had millions of years to work on locating the *Uluspansa*—years during which the scattered bands of subhuman savages would hardly have impeded us—and no trace of the old civilization would now remain. Humanity—you, Jared Hiller—could not have stumbled onto the *Uluspansa* at a worse time. Earth is on the brink of total population crisis once again, and now, as before, the Eridani star system is the nearest that is actually favorable to life. Our own ships ventured far enough from Eridani in past centuries, before interest in exploration declined, to verify that there are no other habitable planets within a radius of twenty parsecs. And now Earthmen have the faster-than-light ships that can bring them here—their short life spans are no longer a barrier. Soon other *Uluspansa* that we were unable to find will yield themselves to the extensive searches of your government. Soon, some brilliant archaeologist will light the fuse."

Hiller watched without seeming to as the barrel of the blaster swung to punctuate each point.

"Earth's technology is still inferior to ours, but it grows stronger and more advanced by the day, especially in the arts of violence and destruction. That is why the solution must come now, and that is why this time it must be final." She looked at him, her eyes full of entreaty. "Can you understand that? Now that you know, can you see it from our perspective?"

"I can see why the council might view it that way," he said. "I can also see why they are wrong; totally and fatally wrong."

"What do you mean, fatally?"

He shook his head. "Annie, my love, it's time we had an understanding. What happens to me when you call in your friends?"

Her feet shifted uncomfortably. "You'll be taken into custody."

"I dislike euphemisms."

"It's no euphemism. You'll be treated with every possible courtesy. You have given us what we needed, even though you would rather have died. We respect your loyalty and the council has no reason to be vindictive. When it's all over, I'm sure I can get you released—under certain conditions."

"Into your custody?" Hiller shifted the right leg back and under him. There was one chance left for Earth and he would have to take it now.

"Would that really be so awful?" she asked. "Jared, I have something to tell you—I should have before, but I couldn't; not until you knew everything." Her eyes fell. "It concerns us. . . ."

Hiller struck.

Twenty-six

He awoke on a bed in a small windowless cell with the sense that many hours—perhaps even days—had passed. The base of his skull above the medulla ached and his arm and leg were stiff. He tried to roll onto his right side and realized with a shock that the arm was gone—sheared off at the shoulder, leaving a blackened metal stump. Nausea gripped his throat, then passed as he forced himself into psychological distance from the lost arm. It was never a part of his body; never a part . . . Thinking about Anne helped. Was she a good shot, or had she meant to kill him? It didn't matter. Only one thing mattered now. He sat for a moment on the edge of the bed and collected the trailing threads of consciousness which had been severed by the blaster. By now Eridani had probably struck at the co-ordinates he had given them. If things had somehow gone wrong, war could be raging at this very moment all over Earth. Spurred by images of citydomes bursting open and people choking in the foul air or burning in the wash of lasbombs, Hiller stood and felt a tug on top of his head accompanied by sudden giddiness. Reaching up, he probed gingerly through matted hair; felt ice in his stomach when he found the thing; from the center of a shaven circle it thrust upward out of his skull—a slim shaft of metal. Fighting another wave of nausea, he fumbled upward along the shaft, felt the trailing wires; whirled and saw where the lines exited through the wall. He'd seen the cons back on Earth—even psychopathic murderers worked the mines with dull-eyed complacence, made docile by a sliver of metal buried in the cerebral cortex. He rummaged through his own mind. Where had they planted it? What had it done to him? *Under certain conditions,* Anne had said. Under certain conditions he could be released into her custody.

He found where the wires were plugged into the shaft and jerked them out. Then he searched the wall until he found the tiny buried listening device.

"Tell Kotyro I have to see him," he said into it. "Tell him it is of vital importance—that it involves the survival of this planet." His voice sounded strange to him, as though he had not used it for a long time. He was about to repeat the message when a section of wall slid open and Sarko, flanked by a yellow-suited guard, entered the cell. There was a blaster in Sarko's hand; Hiller nodded inwardly at the alien's shrewdness: he had chosen an Earth weapon—one that had just burned away Hiller's arm—rather than a Protep device, which would not arouse as much fear. . . .

"Ah, my dear Hiller; I see you are awake."

"How long have I been out?" Hiller demanded.

"And you have picked up the language beautifully, too," Sarko added. "I knew you had a receptive mind."

Hiller stared at him. *Picked up the language?* Then he realized that he had indeed spoken in Protep, as fluently as if he had been born to it. He glanced at the wires trailing out of the wall, then back at Sarko. "How long have I been out?" he repeated in English.

Sarko clucked to himself. "How stubborn you are. You must learn to adapt."

"How . . ."

"All right; all right. You have been semiconscious for two days. The language programming goes much more smoothly without conscious interference. Now that you have the language, we are ready to proceed with more specific things." Sarko motioned to the guard, who stepped forward and took Hiller by the arm.

"What I said about Eridani is true," he said as Sarko walked over to the wall and picked up the wires.

"It was unwise, pulling these out," Sarko murmured. "You could have injured yourself. Believe me, it will be much simpler if you co-operate, but frankly I do not care if you do. I am quite prepared to kill you if you try anything foolish."

"You don't listen very well."

"What is there to listen to? Your threats are idle. The co-ordinates you gave us have been deciphered and at this very moment the great fleet is striking Allied Command with the full might of Eridani. Soon there will be no more Earth, and you will either learn to live here or you will not live at all."

"I demand to see Kotyro."

"You demand! Kotyro is in council, awaiting the news of Earth's destruction. He is not to be called out at the whim of prisoner scum."

"Then I'll speak to Anne Cantrell."

Sarko rasped merrily deep in his throat. "He would speak to the one who put him here," he said to the guard. "I wonder what he would say to her?"

Hiller turned to the guard. "This creature is mad. If you do not do as I say, your planet is doomed and it will be on the heads of both of you." The guard stared at him impassively. Sarko thrust the blaster under Hiller's chin and forced his head back.

"Mad, am I? We shall see who is mad after your next treatment. It will be a great pity, of course, but some cannot survive the sudden changing of their cerebral potentials. Sometimes the current is too great and the relevant tissues are burnt out—accidentally, of course." Keeping the point of the blaster under Hiller's jaw, Sarko reached up with the wires.

Filled with desperation, Hiller felt his body taking over; knew that it was suicide. He twisted, throwing a shoulder into Sarko and jerking his arm free. The blaster hissed, sending agony through Hiller's left shoulder. He and Sarko screamed together, a nightmare sound; then the alien toppled to the floor, half his face blown away.

Twenty-seven

Hiller crashed against a wall; straightened. The guard was on his knees staring at Sarko, his eyes wide with shock. Stumbling over Sarko's body, he ignored the guard and groped for the blaster. His shoulder was turning numb and his fingers closed awkwardly on the butt of the weapon; when he straightened he found he could only lift his arm at the elbow. It would be enough, but if the arm gave out . . .

Hiller ran through the doorway and found himself in a long corridor; he remembered the mosaic in the floor from the other time he was in the citadel. Good. The council chamber should be nearby. He had difficulty keeping his balance as he hurried down the hallway. A warm wetness spread down his chest and the stench of charred flesh hit his nostrils but he kept his eyes raised—he couldn't afford to go into shock now. Rounding a corner, he almost collided with a small gray-robed Protep, who stepped back with a gasp. Hiller angled the blaster upward from the hip.

"Where is the council chamber?" His voice was a distant snarl in his ears.

"I . . . I . . ."

"Quickly!"

"This way."

He followed the Protep down several more corridors and then stood at last before a high arching doorway.

"Open it."

"Sir, I beg of you . . ."

"Now!"

The Protep obeyed, trembling, and Hiller pushed past him into a huge room with vaulted ceiling and descending circular rows of thronelike chairs, each seating a richly dressed figure. In the center, on a massive column which soared high above the rings of seats, sat a single majestic creature robed in purple. A hush descended and every eye swiveled toward Hiller as he backed into a defensive position against the wall; a muscular human-looking Protep who had been standing before one of the outer thrones, cut off his address and sank into his seat.

"What is the meaning of this?" The voice boomed with rich deep resonance from the column in the center and Hiller blinked up at the creature through the film of tears that blurred his eyes. The speaker looked something like a Protep but was taller, and even slimmer. The skin was a deep indigo color and the huge skull was not bare, but covered with a thick mane of blue-white hair. Hiller stared back at the black wells of the eyes, so deep that not even a fleck of the whites showed.

"Who are you?"

"I am Cvirko, Lord of the Council and of this planet from its beginnings."

An icy hand gripped Hiller's stomach. Could this creature truly be one of the original colonists—a being whose life had spanned twelve million years? He remembered what Anne had said about successive stages of development.

"Jad!"

Hiller's head jerked around and he saw Anne running toward him around the outer fringe of the council chamber. She looked very different in the robe of glowing yellow. The soft brown hair was pulled back from her neck to ride in elegant coils above her head and even at this distance he could sense the regal aura that seemed to emanate from her.

"Stop!" he commanded, and she obeyed instantly, the gown swirling forward around her feet.

"Jad, you must not . . ."

"Shut up."

"Why have you come here, Jared Hiller?" Cvirko's voice seemed preternaturally commanding—almost Godlike, and Hiller had to remind himself that he was facing a human being, who had grown from an embryo just as he had. He tightened his finger on the reassuring bulk of the blaster. Even a twelve-million-year-old being could not live with his chest blown away.

"I have come to save your people and mine."

"How touching," Cvirko said, and a ripple of laughter eddied around the chamber. "As to your world, I fear you have come too late; we have just received word that the site of your Allied Command beneath the Sahara Desert has been totally destroyed."

"Then perhaps you have also learned that the Allied Command is not located there."

Every face in the chamber seemed to freeze; every gesture stilled as though suspended in amber. Hiller heard a buzzing in his ears which came and went. He gritted his teeth . . . must hang on a little longer.

"For what purpose is this lie? The co-ordinates are the ones you gave us. Our ship instruments clearly confirmed the existence of a large underground cavity at those co-ordinates. When you stood on the bridge of the *Hound* one of our colleagues with a special talent was just below you. He has assured us that you sincerely believed you were saving your planet."

"And so I did," Hiller replied, "but those were not the co-ordinates of the base. The area you have just destroyed was a dummy setup—as genuine as the transmitter you used to trick me. If the message had truly been sent, it would have been relayed by automatic boosters to the actual command center, via shielded underground cable. You see, I followed basic procedure, drilled into every agent." Hiller looked around at the staring faces. "It does not matter that the message was not sent. You have sent it for me, by hitting the decoy."

A tall figure near the center stood up angrily. Hiller recognized Kotyro. "Impossible!" the former ambassador snapped. "Lord Cvirko, this man is very devious . . ."

"Hiller speaks the truth." The second speaker was a slender

Protep with dark blue skin and a light fuzz of hair on the great skull—an advanced developmental stage, Hiller guessed. It must be the one who had tried to read his mind earlier on the *Hound*. He shivered.

"Thank you, Kitrink. Sit down, Mr. Ambassador." Kotyro slumped back to his seat, shaken. Cvirko returned his gaze to Hiller. "You have cost us much, but the end will be the same. Your Earth cannot hope to prevail."

"Perhaps, but how many in this room will die? Even now a full Earth fleet is converging on Eridani. You may be able to stop most of them, but if even one gets through . . ." Hiller paused, blinked slowly to clear away the tears, and pressed his back against the wall. The periphery of his vision was edging inward, the numbness in his shoulder spreading. Soon his hand would drop and they could pluck the blaster from his loose fingers. It wouldn't matter then, he knew. He was dying.

"It would be a shame," he said, forcing the waning power of his body into his voice, "to live for twelve million years and then die in a needless war that you yourself have created."

"We have no choice," Cvirko replied. "The direction of your people has been clear for centuries; they will soon be too powerful for us, in the sheer force of their numbers; and they will know. What do you think they will do, Jared Hiller, when they realize the truth about us? Your history is full of pogroms visited upon entire races of your own people by others who have been inflamed against them. What will the hate-mongers and xenophobes do with the knowledge from the *Uluspansa*?"

"It doesn't have to be the way you fear. . . ."

"We cannot afford to take that chance."

"You cannot afford anything else. If you destroy us, you will begin the era of your own extinction." There was a restless stir around the edges of the chamber where the younger, human-looking Proteps sat.

"What do you mean?" demanded a young woman across the chamber.

"You will be silent, Riis. I speak for the council."

"Perhaps you have spoken for them too long," Hiller said.

"Maybe you should explain to your people how the efforts of your scientists to cure their infertility are doomed to failure." It was a calculated stroke—everything he had theorized about the planet hinged on it being correct. The signs were all there—small population, lack of children, the exhibit in the museum. It had to be, but if he was wrong . . .

"Take him out," Cvirko commanded. Hiller tugged upward on the blaster—a few older Proteps near the center began to edge toward him, but first one and then others of the younger ones began to stand. They were the ones who still looked like young Earth people—the ones who had not yet passed into the most radical developmental change since their births.

"Let him speak," cried one. Then another and another joined in, their shouts echoing off the vaulted ceiling in a swelling chorus. Cvirko stood atop the column, a majestic figure glowering over the chamber. Finally he raised his hands and the din subsided.

"If you are fools enough to listen to this viper, then I will not prevent you. Remember, though, the source of your continued breath." The younger ones sat down again and Hiller looked at Cvirko, shocked at the openness of his threat. Somehow this ancient creature controlled the immortality drug; was not afraid to use it as a club. Desperately Hiller projected his voice into the silence.

"One by one you will all exceed the maximum bearing age." He saw the thrust strike home and remembered the withered sexless body of Sarko; the alien's remark that he was neither male nor female. "Then there will be no more chances," he continued. "Eridani will never see one more of you than now exists, and each passing year it will see fewer. How many centuries will it be before the last of you is gone, felled by accident or perhaps . . ." A new thought struck Hiller. He gazed around the chamber looking for other Proteps who looked like Cvirko—others of the original colonists. He could find only about fifty with the same indigo skin and silver hair. " . . . or perhaps even brought down by his own hand," he finished, "like Tuoro—Ilise's guardian? Tell me, Cvirko, are these fifty all that remain of the original three hundred? How many of the rest took their own lives?" The hush in the chamber was absolute; Hiller could read the truth of his words in their faces. For a moment Cvirko was as immobile as the rest, then he stirred and spoke.

"Who are you to question our scientists with your guesses? Even now they near a solution."

"You would leave the problem of fertility in the hands of ancients who have passed the bearing age?"

"They will find the solution."

"There is only one solution." Hiller looked at Anne and their eyes locked while a murmur went round the chamber and died.

"What is it, Jared?"

"Earth and Eridani must interbreed."

There was an immediate babble among the inner circles and Cvirko stood, sweeping his robes in front of him. "For that obscenity I will have your tongue removed. To suggest that our pure blood be mingled with the disease and mutation-ridden ooze of your wild species is worse than bestiality." There was a buzz of agreement among the elders but Hiller saw that the younger members were silent; some watching him thoughtfully. "We have had agents on Earth sterilized and banished for attempting such a blasphemy. Sarko, with whom you are acquainted, lost his own son to the vile perversion, and you call it a solution."

Hiller felt the touch of understanding; saw the Inquisitor's hatred in the new light. "It is the only solution," he said quietly. "Your blood is pure all right—so pure after millenniums of inbreeding that it's as lifeless as water, for all your immortality. That child, in the museum. It was your last, wasn't it?"

Cvirko did not reply.

"Yes," Anne said softly. "The last in two hundred years. It lived for eighteen months and then died for no reason."

"It's been in front of you all this time," Hiller said, "but your minds have been closed by millions of years of fear and prejudice. Those ships outside your spaceports—how long have they sat idle because there are barely enough of you to inhabit one planet, let alone the universe? How many years did you limit your breeding to just enough for this one planet before your breeding began to limit you? Is this the price you will pay for your eternal lives—an eternity of stagnation on a single world? I have seen your culture: it's indolent, jaded. It searches for its dreams in drugged stupors. It's no wonder your ancients destroy themselves rather than face an infinity trapped between their boredom and their fear. Perhaps in the end you will be afraid to step from your houses for fear a tree might fall on you."

"I will listen to no more of this. Seize him."

No one moved.

"Look at them," Hiller said. "You've held the secret of eternal life above their heads for too long. They have no stomach for seizing me. Can't you see it, Lord Cvirko? Earth and Eridani need each other to survive. We need your knowledge, your vast experience, your help, instead of your resistance, so that we can reach the stars. You need our vigor, the vitality of our unpredictable genes, the influx of ideas to revitalize minds which have run far too long in the same tracks. Together we, the full human race, can have the galaxy—the universe. It's the only place big enough for an immortal man. Apart, we die."

A young Protep burst into the chamber. Hiller tried to cover him with the blaster, but his arm sank down and the weapon clattered to the floor. The newcomer ignored him.

"Lord Cvirko, members of the council," he shouted breathlessly, "an Earth fleet has gone into hyperspace—they are headed for our planet!"

Cvirko's voice powered over the sudden hubbub. "I gave a command; seize that man!"

The chamber grew still again. A few yellow-suited men moved forward and Hiller watched them dumbly.

"Stop!" Anne's voice rang out. Every eye turned toward her. "Hiller is right, you must listen to him."

"My child," the ancient lord of the Proteps began, "you don't know what you're saying . . ." He motioned again to the guards and she ran to Hiller's side, interposing herself between them.

"Will you murder the man who has already fathered your own blood?" She turned to Hiller, her eyes pleading. "I tried to tell you, Jad; on the *Hound,* but you jumped me and the blaster went off. . . ." The chamber stood aghast. Cvirko sat down slowly. Hiller peered through the deepening haze into Anne's eyes, and the last thing he heard was the raucous sound of his own laughter.

Twenty-eight

(*Epilogue*)

Captain Jared Hiller, U.P.S.N., sat on the bridge and watched the universe cluster into the forward viewscreen as the *Aldebaran* attained hyperlight speed. The crushing pressures of acceleration were bled entirely into the two-foot space between the inner and outer hulls through a feat of engineering invented on Eridani two years after the Great Reunion, as politicians and historians were already calling it. Hiller did not understand how the process worked, but he had not understood the now obsolete Opperman drive principle either. Perhaps in a century or so he would take time out to study it. He reached out with his right hand to activate the course display board and knew a moment of simple and private pleasure as his overlong fingernails clicked against the switch. The Protep physicians who had restored his arm, leg, and eye from small cultures of his germ plasm had offered to inhibit the growth of his nails permanently, but he had refused. Somehow it seemed important to let them grow. He activated the screen and let his fingers dwell for a moment on the smooth plastic of the switch while he calculated the next jump for the sixth time. His obsessiveness did not bother him; it was the way of command, and he would do it even if the lives of three hundred colonists and fifty-two crew did not depend on him.

He flicked the screen off again and looked contentedly around the massive bridge. It was good to be in space again after seven long years as Chief Intermediary. He let his mind touch back on those years as his eyes roamed automatically around the crew stations. The first months had been the hardest—not because of the third-degree burns on his shoulder, which had been healed in an incredible thirty minutes after Cvirko had made up his mind, but from what had come next. The two fleets had hung poised for weeks outside the orbit of Eridani's larger moon while he shuttled back and forth between Admiral Petrov and Lord Zinzikus, using his newly acquired facility in the Protep language. Finally "Old Bloodyboots" Petrov and his equally crusty counterpart had broken off the showdown and repaired to their home planets, presaging summit talks between Lord Cvirko and the World Procurator. Diplomatic missions were set up on both worlds and the long process of admixture began a year later with the first emigration programs. There was still much suspicion and bigotry on both sides, especially on the home planets, but as he looked around now at his collection of Protep and Terran crewmen, Hiller was happy to leave the slower pressures of rationality to do at home what necessity had already dictated on his ship. The intercom buzzed at his wrist and he depressed a button on the side of the armrest.

"Captain speaking."

"Daddy, can I come up on the bridge?"

Hiller smiled at the childish enthusiasm in Jaime's voice. "Sure, honey."

There was an excited chatter out of range of the pickup and then the intercom went dead. Hiller settled back in his chair, a feeling of pleasure spreading through him. She was a sharp kid, his Jaime, and good-looking, like her mother. He remembered with a smile that climactic moment when both he and Jaime's many-times-great grandfather, Cvirko, had learned that Anne held in her womb the first Protep conception in two hundred years. He had wondered many times since just how big a part that *fait accompli* had played in Cvirko's decision. The old ruler had insisted ever since that it was the ultimate good of his people that had led him to break off the ill-started war with Earth. Perhaps.

Jaime clattered onto the deck followed by Anne, and Hiller had to suppress the feeling of wrongness at having civilians on the bridge that persisted from the old days.

"Hi, sweetheart," he said, mussing the soft brown hair.

"Hi, Daddy." She looked around for her friend Shrilenka, who was the *Aldebaran*'s chief survey officer. When they got to Rigel IV, he would become a very busy man, but now he enjoyed nothing more than amusing his captain's daughter with Protep fairy tales. Hiller turned to Anne.

"How are the colonists?"

"Not a whimper. They're as excited as school children." She laid a hand on his shoulder and he covered it briefly with his own. Jaime ran around the bridge looking into the side viewports; they watched as she returned to them with a dejected frown. Hiller knew why she was disappointed; as they hurtled forward at superlight velocity, the universe appeared to foreshorten in the direction of the prow so that all the stars seemed to crowd together in front of them. From all the other viewscreens one could see only black and empty space.

"Daddy, where are all the stars?"

"Ahead of us, Jaime," Hiller said. "Ahead of us."